This is a work of fiction. Similarities to re
are entirely coincidental.

THE PALESTINE MUSEUM

First edition. January 18, 2024.

ISBN: 979-8223319498

Written by Uri Marcus Hes.

The Palestine Museum

Politically Engaged Stories

Uri Marcus Hes

Translated from the Hebrew original by the author

CONTENTS

A Note to the Reader

Regardless of the fact certain historical personalities appear in the following stories, the author has no journalistic intentions, and the featured characters are used as purely fictional ones.

The reader is advised to check historical accuracy of events independently and attach no documentary importance to the stories.

All distortions in conveying actual facts by the author are to be viewed as artistic license.

Historical references may be suggested in the footnotes, which accompany certain stories.

Restless

He who in Amsterdam sought "Jerusalem"
And opened up to Jerusalem, like a clam
Once in Jerusalem, he murmured fervently
Amsterdam, Amsterdam
Loose translation from the Dutch by UMH
Onrust, Jacob Israel de Haan, 1921.

Indeed, he was restless, like in the title of his poem. His sister Lea—only a year, less two months, his junior—had also described him as such. Both were excellent authors. They grew up in an orthodox Jewish family, survivors, together with five other brothers and sisters, of a fraternity of eighteen. Their progenitor, in order to support the large family, had to accumulate a number of part-time jobs, as teacher, maintenance worker and cantor. Regardless of all this, life in the Netherlands was more than adequate for them all, as the children themselves stated on various occasions.

So why, in fact, did Jacob de Haan leave Europe for Palestine in 1904?

Merely because he was restless.

The story I am about to share was told only indirectly, and usually to an audience of religious Jews, not a secular one. If I feel the necessity to narrate it now, it is not out of guilt or shame, God forbid, but out of a deep sense of awe: that the Almighty's ways are hidden from us, and that seemingly crooked lines straighten up in the end.

Jacob's father was a pious man, but hot-tempered. Of the seven brothers and sisters, Jacob was the most defiant. During his youth he was attracted to various radical movements in the Netherlands, from avant-garde artist and poet groups to communist ones. In order to punish him for his rebelliousness, one day his father called him *heretic, pervert, Cain*. Jacob could not return to his parents' home afterward. That hurt him terribly; he was very close to both his mother and sister Lea (Carry). Regardless of hardships, Jacob managed to complete his studies, become an attorney, write and publish poetry and fiction as well as practice law. Still, he remained restless.

Jacob already knew Hebrew through his religious studies as a youngster in Holland, but his accent and intonation were not those of the East European Jewish immigrants, the Zionists active in Palestine. He did not have the elbows and roughness of those native to Odessa. No one accepted him as a political or legal adviser: he was offered gardening or construction roadwork instead. Notwithstanding, being resourceful, he managed to make a living as a correspondent for a number of foreign papers. To satisfy his sexual needs he would visit occasionally the in-wall sectors of the old city.

Where do I fit into all this?

On the surface, I had no part whatsoever in the story. I grew up in a conventional Zionist family in Jerusalem and had no unusual tendencies or even a strong need to rebel. Unlike Jacob Israel de Haan, I was not restless. Mine was a generation that came after the British mandate. If anything binds de Haan and me, it is the strong wish to see eventually a place for the weak in their struggle against the powerful, or a kind of belief in higher morals, a step above the daily bickering of the city governors and bureaucrats. And yet, destiny had it so that life's paths brought de Haan story and my own together.

My father was one of the Hagannah's[1] main commanding officers. I have never heard the name de Haan referred to in our home, or perhaps only in the context of the national poet Bialik, who had once quoted some of de Haan's verses. My mother was a great poetry fan, and I might have inherited some of this inclination. Chanting was another soft spot of mine, and I would furtively listen to the cantor praying in the Nakhla'ot Persian synagogue next door to where we lived. This weakness of mine was not to be mentioned openly, as our parents were ferociously secular. Even Sephardic Jews were not to be overly praised, as they bore a strong resemblance to Arabs. In this respect, it must be admitted, I was a bit of a rebel, but no one—not even my mother—was aware of my defiance.

The period of the British mandate, with its outbursts of Arab resistance, was now behind us. I was—we were—the generation born with the State. My father was considered a hero and a founding stone of the impressive Israeli Defense Forces. But without any warning, he had a heart attack at the age of fifty-four or fifty-five. I was still in the Rehavia high school. It was hard to acknowledge that someone that represented resistance and strength could all of a sudden lose all his force and collapse in the open terrace of our home. Several years earlier, we had moved to an apartment on Keren Hayesod Street, and at that moment were watching the Independence Day parade from the balcony.

Only when a Red Shield of David ambulance came to get my father and take him to the Sharei Tsdek Hospital did my mother cry all of a sudden, "Not to that hospital, not to that hospital," insisting that the paramedics accompany my dad to the Hadassah Hospital a bit farther away. It is then that I recalled Father was a heavy smoker, who had frequent coughing spells. Two days later, when he returned home and said the attack was light and not life-threatening, Father was still strolling around with a cane. He took me nonetheless to the entrance parlor of our home—one which served both as an improvised office and a radio room—and said there was something he had to share with me. Despite the fact his life was not in danger, he told me, one day it might be. In case he was ever accused of having acted illegally, he continued, it would be important that he be covered, or "one-hundred-percent covered" as he emphasized. My father held a tiny safe, like those metal boxes used in the Edison Cinema by ticket vendors, and opened it with a small key and pulled out a paper note. A simple notebook page, which did not even seem old or remarkable.

"If you are ever told your father acted illegally in the de Haan case," he told me, "you could always present this page. It is signed by the present president of the State of Israel and proves your dad was not a murderer."

I was sixteen years old, but for a brief moment I felt like an insecure infant. Not only had my father, a fierce soldier and commander, undergone a stroke and been taken to the hospital but now suddenly he was also accused of murder. This was how I came to hear of the de Haan killing.

It was not only the Arab population that was an obstacle to the Zionist settlement project in Palestine but its old-time Jewish population as well, on the whole a highly orthodox one. These Jews did not seek a state of their own and reminded the newly arrived Zionist settlers too much of the Jews left behind in Eastern Europe, that part of the world the Zionists wished to forget.

An attempt on the life of Rabbi Sonnenfeld, head of the Orthodox Jewish community, had already preceded the killing of de Haan, not by some extreme revisionists or something similar but by members of the mainstream Hashomer movement. Rabbi Sonnenfeld was a friendly, open-minded person, who wished to live in peace with the Palestinian Arabs. The attempt on his life was aborted only by chance, so the threat to the Orthodox community remained.

Jacob de Haan found his way back to Orthodox Judaism only gradually, after numerous doubts and hesitations. The religious Mizrahi movement, which he had known back in the Netherlands, tried to integrate into the dominant Zionist organization, so de Haan affiliated himself with the more religious, old-time residents of Jerusalem, the Orthodox Jews.

Because of his vast experience in jurisprudence, and his knowledge of English, German and French, de Haan was able to assist Rabbi Sonnenfeld in his struggle for the independence and equal rights of the Orthodox community. The Zionist politicians, with their military bodies of the Shomer and the Hagannah, did not appreciate such partisanship. Threats on the life of de Haan did not take long to arrive.

From 1923 onward, de Haan received anonymous menacing letters in Hebrew. An actual visit of warning by the Hagannah left no doubt that his life was in danger. The British authorities recommended de Haan arm himself or get some protection, but he refused. The only obvious explanation for that refusal was that de Haan was restless.

A day prior to de Haan's journey to London, on behalf of the old Jewish communities of Palestine, he left the house as usual for evening prayers. These were held in the Sharei Tsedek synagogue of Jerusalem, just by the hospital on Jaffa Street. Two armed men awaited him in the darkness. As soon as he finished praying, they shot de Haan three times. Both were Hagannah members, one of them my dad.

The year I found out about de Haan, I left the Masada Boy Scouts and asked to join the observant Bnei Akiva youth movement. It did not occur to me that I would have to become religious first, and the youth leader's reaction surprised me. When I realized I had to officially convert, as it were, it became clear to me that the cotton knitted head covering of the Bnei Akiva did not interest me at all. It was the ultra-religious hats and skullcaps I was drawn to. I joined an Orthodox yeshiva and from then on had little contact with my family. Life is a narrow bridge one ought to cross watchful about every pitfall. This is the meaning of being observant: those that watch their very step.[2]

On the last occasion I saw my father, he made a point of telling me the page from that little metal box was removed and deposited in "safe hands," somewhere in the United States. "Such a note could become explosive in the hands of someone like you," he said, gesturing to my hat and black overcoat, without spelling out *observant Jew*. It is obvious to me now: if my father had decided to kill de Haan, when the latter was about to represent the old religious Jews of Jerusalem in London, it was because he too was restless.

A Last Month

Not without discomfort, one has to admit, it was neither in Arabic nor Hebrew that Alter and Khalil conversed but in English. In an almost epic experience, like the one of Alter and Khalil, a story about mutual understanding and hope for a peaceful future, it would have been nice to report that their two languages merged. What might come as a comfort is the fact that certain exclamations, swearwords and curses were indeed in Arabic or Hebrew—but of course other linguistic variants in Turkish, German and Russian made their way to the surface as well. So I am forced to say the effect of this comfort is quite limited.

It shouldn't astound one that two cultivated gentlemen, who carefully constructed their sentences and selected the proper idioms in Shakespeare's tongue, allowed themselves the use of foul language. Those were difficult times then, and the situation they found themselves in was extreme. The year was 1917. It was the last month of the last year of the war, and as the British army advanced the last Ottoman soldiers were evacuating Jerusalem. Alter and Khalil, a Jewish poet and an Arab poet, found themselves prisoners of the retreating forces. The one's left arm was tied in a dirty flax rope to the other's right, watched over by Turkish guards on horseback. They had been arrested the previous evening and expelled from Palestine to serve a sentence in the dark dungeons of Damascus. Now, the four-hundred-kilometer walk on rugged roads lay ahead of them. In their place I, no doubt, would have cursed my fate as well.

"Ah," said Khalil, "there is nothing like a cold trickle of water to begin the day with, and the more so if poured out of an earthenware jug. "

"Personally," Alter replied, "I would have preferred a hot cup of coffee..."

"Away with those European habits!" Khalil exclaimed. "This is the true existence. Had you woken early enough in my home, when you were visiting, you would have noticed how, every morning, I took a cold shower and went for a brisk walk. Before I even sat down to breakfast."

"With the madness of our arrest yesterday, I did not get much sleep. I hope my agitation did not cause you to stay up, as well, Khalil."

"Seeing the city in flames, with bombs falling around us, was indeed awful," Khalil said, "but the forced march from town allowed me to fall asleep more easily."

Alter watched as some riders overtook them and commented, "The soldiers are joking as if they were on a field trip. They, at least, had a good night's sleep..."

"Soldiers are soldiers," Khalil replied, "and don't forget that, for them, it is the big journey home."

"Istanbul, Damascus, Jerusalem," Alter complained, "how did it help the Ottomans to construct an impressive rail line if, now humiliated, they are struggling to make their way home with packs on their backs?"

"At least they are mounting horses and not on foot," Khalil pointed out.

Only one or two riders, who needed to stretch their limbs and get some circulation back, climbed down for a walk from time to time. Other guards and soldiers were carried on mule carts.

"Wasn't it King Richard who offered his entire kingdom in exchange for a horse?"

"Poor Richard," Alter replied. "Just like us he had to quit Jerusalem in shame...or am I getting the two Richards confused?"

"Richard the Crusader lived some three hundred years before Shakespeare's Richard III," Khalil said. "But he, too, was desperate for a horse. Every Arab child in my school is taught that the triumphant Saladin still offered Richard the Lion Heart a noble horse to ride upon."

"Ah, that is right," Alter replied. "It was the famous Richard Coeur de Lion that befriended Saladin and his brother..."

After some hesitation Khalil said, "For the Muslims, he was more infamous than famous. In Ascalon, for example, he killed the entire population. But history constantly changes. The very path we are treading is a Roman road. Where are they today? The Crusaders, too, whose monastery we shall pass by shortly, have gone. Now we are accompanying the Ottomans' retreat. This land is an open history text."

"But the friendship between King Richard and the Saladins," Alter asks, "was that not an example of true coexistence? They even agreed to share Palestine between them!"

"My dear Alter," Khalil replied, "they might have signed the Ramla treaty, but Richard had to make do with a thin strip of shore, between Atlit and Jaffa. Such a treaty I would be glad to grant you any day. But will you Zionists be content with that? *Inshallah!*"

Khalil and Alter had spent the previous night in Khan Al Akhmar, a three-hour walk from Jerusalem. Today, together with the last group of cavalry and the remaining soldiers and guards, they made the steep descent below sea level in the direction of the Dead Sea. The sun above bore no resemblance to a European December sun: it hit their heads relentlessly. As prior to leaving Jerusalem, Alter and Khalil had prepared themselves for an intense winter in Damascus, they were now overdressed: sweat poured down their bodies. In their dusty shoes and with empty stomachs, they arrived at an impressive structure, all arches, solitary in the dry desert. The Turkish riders attached their horses to heavy metal rings, placed around a large open patio. The old guard, who was meant to surveil Alter and Khalil, led them to a fly-infested side building, where some poor-looking police officials and soldiers stood lost in the shade. By a fountain, their hands still attached, Alter and Khalil tried to wash themselves, each of them whispering thanks, as well as some prayers, that preceded the meal.

It occurs to me, that not only swearwords but blessings and exclamations as well were recited in the mother tongues. Perhaps these were the fundamental emotions, those stemming from the heart, which retained their Arabic and Hebrew form. But this is just speculation on my part.

Alter and Khalil observed the old police guard distancing himself from the building to urinate against a lone cypress tree. The man and the tree seemed to exist in another time and age, just barely perceived, in the haze of the midday heat.

In the shade, heavily salted goat cheese and cucumbers were given to them.

"The salt of the earth," Khalil mumbled, and after a while he said to Alter, "Prior to Easter, or your Passover, Arabs come to this place to celebrate the prophet Moses. To Christian Arabs, it is a time of fasting and mourning. Here in the area, Jesus meditated all alone in the desert, preparing himself for his last days."

Their day was not yet over. Alter and Khalil still had some thirteen kilometers more to walk in the scorching sun. After an hour or so, they perceived the Saint George monastery in the distance. Not far from them, the Roman aqueduct carried water, whose gushing sound they were able to hear. Both soldiers and guards were permitted to wash in the chilly water of a cement basin. Even the horses received a scrub and a spray.

"I am half dried-up, and these sons of bitches splash the horses to cool them down," Khalil muttered. "What a sadistic pleasure, to watch us in this state. Even our own guard has disappeared, and the others won't mind if we drop dead of thirst and exhaustion."

"You took the words right out of my mouth," Alter said. "It's been hours since we were given a gulp of water."

The city of Jericho appeared before them, all green and lush from its many springs. Khalil watched it for a long time before he said, "My parents, in their youth, would come occasionally to Jericho. The Sultan spring was known for its fertility properties, and this is scientific truth!"

Alter smiled and said, "Daring Arab couples..."

"It is likely," Khalil said, "that in this very place I was conceived and, if we are not given water to drink, will also be the place where my days will end..."

"They will not permit you to die so easily, Khalil. You will first have to bear a few months of torture before that pleasure is granted you."

Only toward sunset, all hurting, did they reach the outskirts of the city itself. Exhausted, they trod the narrow lanes, bordered by fruit trees and gardens on both sides. A cool evening breeze reached the stone walls.

"The rousing fragrance of Jericho!" Khalil called out, "What a poetic line!"

Indeed, the perfume of citrus blossom was still in the air.

"Season, season and its scents..." Alter improvised and, inspired by the resemblance of the name Jericho and the words *month* and *moon*, he continued, "In all cultures, man has stood wondering at the moon, its waning and rebirth, twelve times a year. Jericho has probably been named after moon worshippers of old..."

"Even our common ancestor, Abraham, was probably brought up in this tradition. But unlike his forefathers he tried to make a new start and believe in a single God. Jesus and Mohammed followed suit."

From afar, they could discern the Turkish camp, erected only a few hours earlier, and now lit by oil lamps and open fires. Alter and Khalil were shown where they would spend the night and be given something to eat. Before that, arms still attached, they were brought to a mound of sand to relieve themselves and defecate.

"May their homes be destroyed," Khalil said."I was so proud to install a modern shower and toilets in my Jerusalem home. Now I am obliged to empty my bowels in the sand, like a dog."

"We both went through the American hygienic revolution," Alter replies. "Following it, even human sweat is considered barbaric. This experience of ours certainly puts things into perspective."

While maneuvering into sitting down for a meal, Alter mumbled to himself, "This must be considered *Pikuakh Nefesh*..." and louder he said, "In the coming weeks and months, I will transgress, by necessity, the strict rules of my religion—if I am still alive, that is. There is no way for me to observe eating kosher, in our conditions of exile..."

Khalil replied, "You may imagine that this is not a topic I am thrilled to discuss."

"I know perfectly well what you are alluding to, Khalil. I know well that most likely we ended up in this situation because of the kosher food I ordered sent to me, while hiding in your house. But how was I to know Turkish soldiers would follow my mother-in-law when she brought the food? How was I to know the servant lady refused to bring it herself on a Friday?"

"I am not holding you to blame," said Khalil.

Since early that morning they had only been given a few cucumbers and a small cube of salty cheese. Now they were grateful to receive a bun stuffed with ground meat and eggplant. Alter thanked God that Muslims did not eat pork.

In addition to their hands, one of their feet was attached during the night. Khalil and Alter helped each other undo their shoes. The old guard offered to massage their painful joints. "This encourages the blood," he managed to say in Arabic. Back to back, they lay beside the numerous bags which the soldiers unloaded from the horses and carts.

"Perhaps you will outgrow Zionism as a result of this absurd journey," Khalil said to Alter with half a smile.

"My wife became insane after police interrogations. Now I am breaking the rules of my religion, and you wish me to give up my yearnings for Zion as well?" Alter said.

"I have nothing against your family—may Allah grant them long lives and blessings—nor against you eating kosher, Alter. It is the Balfour declaration that bugs me. The English promised to liberate the

Arabs from the Turks. What kind of honor could they still have if they promise our land to the Jews at the same time?"

"If I abandon Zionism," Alter said, "what are you willing to forgo, once we are released?"

"Perhaps I will forgive the British for not keeping their word," Khalil said.

"Let's bend and straighten our tied hands together," Alter suggested, "before we go completely out of our minds, being tied this way..."

"You probably have a week more to get used to it," Khalil replied.

"Did you mean what you said, about not blaming me for the arrest?" Alter wanted to know. "Had you not given me shelter in your home, I would have made this very trip on my own, a Jewish American enemy of the Ottoman Empire, attached to a mule cart, instead of to you."

"If one thing bothers me, and will remain irksome, with or without a Jewish homeland..."

"Yes," said Alter.

"If one thing continues to trouble me, it isn't the arrest itself... What hurt me so deeply was your refusal to share my own food. I would have done everything, even ordered kosher food from the Shief Hotel...but you ordering food, brought to you in my own home, while I was your host. This I could never comprehend."

"I am so ashamed, Khalil," Alter said. "Ashamed, and sorry, from the bottom of my heart."

Following a long silence, Khalil squeezed Alter's hand, the hand attached to his by a rope of flax. Covering themselves as best they could with jute bags left over from the previous citrus harvest, Khalil whispered, "*Tusbakh al kher*," and Alter replied, "May the morning shine upon you, as well, Khalil."

1917 was, perhaps, the last year in which one could remain an optimist, in that part of the world.

The Palestine Museum

1

Jordanian soldiers seized the British High Commissioner's Residence in southern Jerusalem on the 5th of June but lost it hours later to an Israeli unit. The Israelis attacked the museum, located just north of the Old City, with rockets and machine gun fire until a paratrooper unit took it at 7.27am the next day. The solid stone walls, which I knew so intimately, were severely damaged.

I hear all this today in 1967 from the Greek consul to Jerusalem, who faithfully reports to me by telephone here in Athens, where I reside.

Twenty years have passed since the British left Jerusalem, and thirty years have passed since I left the city myself, although it feels like much longer than that. I used to traverse this stretch of land between the Commissioner's Residence and the museum – which has now switched hands – with a horse and cart almost every day. Over fifteen years I learnt to recognise most of the paths that crossed the white and rocky landscape, which was far from being the most hospitable in the world.

At the time, I felt that it was my new home. In fact, a striking number of people felt the same way. Many, perhaps too many, still feel that way today. But few have the magnanimity to share that land with their fellow human beings. It seems to me that it has always been a land of dispute and conflict.

I arrived in Jerusalem right after it was recognised as a British colony. I say 'colony' even though the precise term in the text is somewhat different. During the Great War at the beginning of the century, the British Army managed to take the city from the Turks, who had ruled it for a very long time, and from the Germans, who had held it for only a short period. It seemed, at least initially, that the city's residents were happy to see us.

After four years of world war and the hasty departure of the Germans and the Turks, the city was in quite a depressing state. There was no electricity supply, and even water supply, sewerage services and rubbish collection were sporadic. The railway line that once connected Jerusalem to the outside world was old and had been badly damaged in the fighting. There were almost no cars around, and even fewer roads to drive on.

Representatives of the British government – officials belonging to what had been considered an essentially military local government – welcomed me in typically formal fashion. Soldiers of my age gave me a warmer reception, as did quite a few women, mainly Jewish, who came from all corners of the Middle East and Europe to work in the city's two main brothels. This may not have been the most celebrated aspect of the British colony, but it still allowed for a more direct and vivid acquaintance with the day-to-day spirit of the place.

As my thirteen-year-old adopted grandson enters my living room here in Athens, I will continue to convey things in a more subtle and responsible way, especially since he is showing genuine interest in my recollections of that period.

I decided not to live in one of the official government buildings available to me, or even in one of Jerusalem's many hotels. I believed that if I had to get to know the city and adapt to its way of life, I could not do so in an English military facility or a Viennese-style hotel.

I lived in the neighbourhood of Abu Tor, one of the first non-Jewish neighbourhoods built outside the walls of the Old City. Even then, these neighbourhoods impressed me, as they combined modern construction methods with the local limestone, and adopted or integrated motifs from Turkish or Persian building styles.

The Old City of Jerusalem was charming and impressive, with its narrow and winding alleyways that linked countless squares and dark tunnels, forming a labyrinth. Peddlers, donkeys, sheep and goats crowded the alleyways, which made them nearly impassable. Stalls displaying fabrics, fruits and spices added splashes of red, green and purple to the backdrop of the white stone houses. However, I decided it was impractical to live within the city walls. In the summer the smell of sewage and decay were unbearable, and in the evenings I wanted to roam freely on the hills surrounding the city.

Before I go any further, I ought to say that I arrived in Jerusalem after completing my studies in architecture to take up a contract working with the local government. More precisely, the British mandate authorities in Palestine hired me as their chief architect, although at the time I was only briefly acquainted with the Middle East and had limited professional experience.

The four years of war in Europe, with their mutual massacres, stripped me of any military ambitions, but I remained eager to embark on a new and creative chapter of my life. Jerusalem seemed the most suitable place to realise my professional plans. One person who shared my anti-militaristic ideas was the physicist Albert Einstein, who came to the city to inaugurate the Hebrew University. He stayed with me in my house in Abu Tor. I took him on a tour along the ridge overlooking the Old City, the hills sloping towards the Judean Desert and the Dead Sea Valley. To be honest, I had mixed feelings about him during his visit.

He was of course a man of stature and vision, yet – perhaps due to his heavy German accent and hesitant English – he seemed to me so Jewish and even provincial that I couldn't quite look him in the eye. I felt sheepish about it for, after all, it was I who had invited him to stay in my home. True, there were no decent hotels in Jerusalem at that time – the King David Hotel had not yet opened – but I had expected to find him a bit more ... how should I put it ... sophisticated. Years later, the State of Israel invited him to be its first president. To his credit, he declined, but the invitation itself didn't surprise me. He represented, for me, a brilliant and open-minded man but one a bit too idiosyncratic in his Judaism.

I don't want to sound intolerant or dogmatic, but one of our goals for Jerusalem was to transform it into a truly cosmopolitan city rather than just another provincial town. The idea that the city would develop its own distinct Jewish flavour was, so to speak, a nightmare that became a reality. In hindsight, it's easier to understand how things declined, even though, without being boastful, I was one of the few who warned the government of this eventual development.

2

Instead of offering a historical thesis, as I am not a historian and that is not the purpose of my memoirs, I will describe some of the people around me at that time. Not all of them were impressive or famous like Einstein – most of them remained completely unknown – but all of them played a part directly or indirectly in constructing important buildings, such as the Commissioner's House or the museum, and in shaping the city of Jerusalem as we know it today.

The first amongst these figures was Orde Wingate. Like me, Orde was a British soldier in the service of His Majesty, appointed to serve the Mandate government as an intelligence officer. Like his cousin, the famous T. E. Lawrence (yes, that very Lawrence of Arabia), Orde was brought up in a devout evangelical community. And, like his cousin, he was deeply influenced by a kind of religious fervour, one might say almost of a messianic character, which coloured his entire political outlook and even his military involvement in the Middle East. Moreover, both men had strange tendencies that seemed to stem, at least partially, from their education in English private and military schools, which were considered excellent. For instance, as an officer, Orde would sometimes appear dressed *only* in a pair of standard military boots, holding the Holy Scriptures in one hand.

I do not recount these tales to besmirch Orde's reputation or taint the record of Zionism, but rather to complete the picture given of that period; a reality I experienced for fifteen years and that I am now relating for the sake of future generations. Until his late thirties, Orde refrained from engaging in any sexual relations, as he dedicated his life to a woman he hoped to marry one day. Like the knights of the medieval era, who carried in their hearts the name of a cherished lady and for whom they fought in various battles, Orde sought his way in British settlements and fought for his own interpretation of courtly love.

When I asked him why he chose to defy military regulations and walk around in Adam's attire, he said it was just a military tactic. After all, according to him, the 'barbarians' in the Middle East would sometimes seek to humiliate prisoners of war by stripping them naked or even occasionally cutting off their genitals. I replied that, in *his* case, that might not be such a big loss, given he made so little use of those organs. Later I was told that, in Orde's English military school, recruits had to pull their trousers down and sit in an ice-cold bath as a punishment. In my eyes, this was an example of barbarity in its 'enlightened' British form.

Orde Wingate was consumed by the idea of the Jews' return to the Holy Land. For him, the young Jews of the 'Yishuv', as they called their settlements in Palestine, were the knights of the Kingdom of Heaven. Speaking of Jewish 'knights'... those who were born in Palestine somehow fitted the role despite their decision to wear, of all things, either British khaki or Russian shirts, distinguishing themselves from the white Russians by sporting a red ribbon. Those from Eastern or Central Europe had little in common with chivalry, with their thick glasses, sparse beards and paunches. Why Orde chose to mentor and train them for the British Army's so-called shock units is still beyond me.

I chose to start the story with such an extravagant character to illustrate the odds against which the British government had to struggle in those days. The pressure exerted on it by the Zionist movement was tremendous, but represented only one side of the story; we must not forget the Palestinian leaders and inhabitants. Both Jewish and Arab bodies of various hues helped the British Army overcome the Turkish and German forces during the Great War. The government promised officially to hand over half of the Arab Peninsula to the Hashemite king. So, where did Lloyd George's sudden announcement of a 'Jewish Homeland' in Palestine come from? From that point onwards, things could only have deteriorated, as I saw for myself.

Jerusalem's electricity supply is a concrete example of the British tied hands at the time. Couldn't the British government, with all its connections in Europe, Egypt and the countries neighbouring Palestine, find a solution to the question of electricity in anyone other than Pinhas Rutenberg? The Electric Company he established, despite being called the Palestinian Company, was actually operated by Zionist investors. Rutenberg, together with Ze'ev Jabotinsky, was one of the founders of the British Jewish Legion, which might explain why his company was chosen in the first place. But how could one ignore the fact that at the same time, Jabotinsky and Trumpeldor openly talked about transferring the Arab population of Palestine to the eastern bank of the Jordan? The choice of such companies over time helped create the conflict that Britain had to deal with.

3

Abu Tor overlooks East Jerusalem. The view is breath-taking. The Judean hills are visible through the dust and haze in a kind of undefined purple, yet seem at the same time to recede into the African–Syrian rift. In the evenings, when time was at my disposal, I left this eternal vista for plainer but no less endearing scenery. I would traverse the fields of Ummariyya, with their limestone rock and olive trees, and climb the Talbiya hill. Here were some of the most beautiful houses outside the city walls. Various Talbiya dignitaries sat on their balconies, waving at me. Mr. Salama and Mr Sa'id were often eager to chat, inviting me sometimes to share with them a glass of sweet mint tea. Jerusalem's water has a taste of its own, which one can detect even through the sugar and the green-brown leaves. Behind us, purple and pink bougainvilleas towered over us; they were some of the most beautiful blooming hedges I had ever seen.

In those days, it was difficult for me to connect with people who were not sensitive to this city. Perhaps it was an advantage that few managed to survive there. We knew that urbanization would turn Jerusalem into a mundane agglomerate, but this wasn't something that my social circle wished to witness. Its inhabitants at the time – Christians, Muslims and Jews –were all eccentric in one way or another, and maybe that's why I felt so comfortable there. It seemed that even the wind blowing through it had something eccentric and haunting about it. Apparently, the Arabs called it *Riya wa Awi*, the 'air of the jackals'.

From Talbiya, I would continue, now almost in complete darkness, towards King George Street. There I would eat something – street food or a kofta kebab from one of the stalls – before ending the evening in a European coffeehouse. At weekends, I would find English or French newspapers there, even though they were a few days out of date. This was a way of life I fancied and a place where I could stay forever, provided the locals did not reject us 'incomers', as they were doing for example in Cairo back then.

Did I mention that, on my visit to Cairo before coming to Jerusalem, I found I had a kind of Arab twin brother there? I say this figuratively, of course, but the meeting with Hassan Fathy helped me feel that my place was indeed in the Middle East, even though I didn't particularly like Egypt itself. Hassan Fathy was a few years younger than me, but like me, he was an Orientalist architect and intellectual. Wrapped in camel-hair *jalabiyas*, those loose-fitting, traditional garments of the Nile Valley, we sat on the rooftop of his house, sipping tea from thin glass cups. We shared the same Western training, technical knowledge and inclination to preserve everything organic and vital in Eastern culture. Together, we spent hours both trying to understand the current political situation and analysing the spiritual and material challenges of the time. Years later, the Greek photographer Dimitri Papadimos joined us and documented some of my meetings with Fathy. However, I'm getting ahead of myself, because Dimitri also played an important part in my stage of life 'after Palestine'. Hassan Fathy revealed to me many secrets of Arab construction, not only in a stylistic sense but also in practical terms, such as how to deal with the excess of light and heat. Windows and ventilation openings played a central role in Egyptian construction, especially in the desert regions. In fact, my first acquaintance with the Arab desert was through him.

The decision not to live in a hotel or one of the official British buildings came with its own set of difficulties. Ayuna, who was the housekeeper, did not have the same habits as we do in the West. For instance, even if the rooms were spotless, she had a significantly different approach to food hygiene. I had severe digestive problems after a few of her meals, until I discovered that she used water from our sewage to irrigate the vegetable patch. I decided that we needed a septic ditch at the entrance to the courtyard, which her 19-year-old son dug according to my instructions. Two pipes then led from the ditch to the bottom of the garden. There, a pool with reeds purified the water before it reached the vegetable garden. The main drawback of the plan was the unbearable smell at the entrance to the courtyard. But few came to visit us, so only Ayuna and I had to suffer the inconvenience. We had an abundance of courgettes, tomatoes, onions and cucumbers. Jerusalem's olive oil is excellent, so with a little rice and occasionally minced meat or an omelette, I was in excellent shape.

4

There were almost no Jewish residents in Abu Tor at the time, but my eyes were drawn to one of them, Ofra. She dressed like a British soldier, in khaki and high boots, but added a scarf or even an Arab *keffiyeh*. Although her family, the Neumanns, was German, Ofra had been in Jerusalem since the age of three. She had almost no German accent in English and apparently none in Hebrew either. Ofra was beautiful but more masculine than any European woman I knew, at least in her demeanour. Her audacity and abrasiveness embarrassed me anew each time we met; she would look at me directly and greet me with a somewhat sarcastic 'Hello'. There wasn't a significant age difference between us, but being around her made me feel like I belonged to a different generation, like some Oxfordian dinosaur. It made me think that Britain, despite its naval power and political sagacity, was indeed turning into a dinosaur back then. The spirit of Victorianism, evidently, still prevailed at the beginning of the twentieth century.

How did I end up talking about Ofra? Well, because Arab women in Jerusalem rarely ventured out on their own, except for women trading in the market, or perhaps it was because Arab and Jewish men gathered separately in their own cafes. At the same time, I was distancing myself from the colonialist attitudes of government officials and the childish behaviour of the British soldiers. The Armenian migration and the increasing presence of European intellectuals and scholars in the city encouraged me, should I ever want to start a family in Jerusalem. Either way, Ofra's 'Shalom' every time we met sounded more like 'What, you're still here?'

5

My early years in Jerusalem were uneventful, personally and professionally. Even the political reality led us to believe that we were entering a long period of relative peace that would allow extensive and important construction to get under way. However, the city's general infrastructure required not only precise planning but also financing that became increasingly difficult to secure.

The revelation that Jerusalem would need to be rebuilt with borrowed funds upset me. Britain's economic decline was becoming evident, and the United States – the rising empire – was taking over. Although I tried to deny the fact at the time, Zionist money played a significant role in the whole affair, as in the case of constructing the university I mentioned earlier in the context of Einstein.

I had no connection to the two most imposing building projects in Jerusalem of those years. Jews from Egypt funded the first, and American Catholics' finance and planning funded the second. Everything I learnt about modern Eastern-like building style, I learnt from these two projects. They encapsulated all the good and bad aspects of Orientalist architecture. Let me explain. If anything tarnished the name of Middle Eastern architecture, it was precisely the excess of money and vulgarity of designers like Hoffmeister, who, with their neo-Syrian, neo-Sudanese or pseudo-Byzantine styles, created a building like the King David Hotel. Although it became the social hub of the city in those years, it didn't say much about the architectural quality of the structure.

In contrast, when Lord Palmer laid the cornerstone for the YMCA building, not far from the King David Hotel, we thought we could still present it as a landmark achievement of the British presence in the Middle East. Although the building is stunning in its beauty, we must acknowledge that the project was 100% American.

Two years after I arrived in Jerusalem, the Museum of Islamic Art was established in the vicinity of the Temple Mount. Besides it, there were only two small museums in the city, and there was no central location to store archaeological findings, which were kept in the courtyards of government buildings. Local Zionist activists proposed establishing a cultural centre between the eastern and western parts of the city, near the construction site of the King David Hotel. We preferred something closer to the Old City, which symbolised for us the heart of Jerusalem.

Thereafter, I invested much of my time in planning and building two central structures, which, to this day, remain the most significant of my life. If the government residence, as we called it, officially the High Commissioner's House, represented the practical, diplomatic and military face of the British in the Middle East, the Palestine Museum was supposed to represent its spiritual and universal aspirations. This latter idea connected me, whether I wanted it or not, to the birth of Christianity in the early centuries and its resurgence during the Crusades in the first millennium. In essence, the two projects paralleled for me the palace of Pontius Pilate on the one hand and the Temple of Jerusalem on the other. Even though we never referred to the government residence as a 'palace', we weren't surprised that the public came to call it the 'Palace of the Commissioner'.

6

When I reflect on all that I have read about Jerusalem, from the Holy Scriptures to Dickens, nothing has moved me more than the visit of the Crusaders to the city. When Britain took control of Palestine, it was precisely 800 years after the Vatican recognised the Latin Kingdom's rule over Jerusalem. The Knights Templar liberated the city from the Muslims, at that time, much as we liberated it from the Turks.

I know that the manner in which the above 'liberation' was enacted was not particularly 'Christian' in spirit. Baldwin, who was declared King of Jerusalem, massacred men, women and children as if they were vermin infesting the city. For months, Jerusalem reeked of the rotting corpses of entire families. In a distinctly European manner, as a devout Christian, Baldwin refrained from any sexual contact during the Crusades. Unless I am mistaken, some form of peace and order was restored to the city only with the sovereign that came after him. Then, Muslims were allowed to trade in Jerusalem during the day but not to stay overnight. Foreign Christians had to be invited to settle in Jerusalem, as the massacre left so few inhabitants: Armenians from the north and Syrian Christians were encouraged to immigrate to Palestine, and certain Muslims were persuaded to embrace Christianity.

In any case, when T.E. Lawrence entered Jaffa Gate with General Allenby and his forces, two years before I arrived in Jerusalem, he must have been elated. Had I been in his place, I would have shared the same sentiment: a feeling of spiritually profound intoxication, a moment when the dream, or even the inner vision, connects with an event in reality. Here I was with the ideas of the Round Table, ingrained in me since childhood, with the ideal of King Arthur and biblical stories, entering the city of knights with a mandate from the nations of the world to prepare Palestine for the modern era. In the early twentieth century, I, a new type of knight, equipped with a compass and theodolite, was ready and prepared to change the face of Jerusalem's hills. It is forgotten today that, like me, Lawrence of Arabia was an Arabist and a trained archaeologist who came to the Middle East armed with the same tools to prepare maps for the British Army.

I am astonished at the emotion that overcame me. After all, it had been clear to all government employees since time immemorial that there was no room for personal feelings – be they religious, political or romantic – in any activity during our mandate. Although I have not been in official employment now for thirty years, and have been retired for the past seventeen, the issue of Palestine is still of the utmost sensitivity. In any conversation related to the subject, one must check the origin and affiliation of the person one is talking with, as any mistaken term one uses may bring the conversation to a halt. Even how one refers to the territory in which Jerusalem is situated must be carefully considered: Palestine, Palestina, Eretz-Yisrael or, now, the State of Israel mean different things to different people. In any case, I will just continue recounting my view of the events during my time there.

7

During my early years in Palestine, a powerful earthquake shook the entire region, causing many buildings to collapse or sustain significant damage. Had I been permeated by religious or evangelical sentiments, like many of my acquaintances or the Americans who arrived in Jerusalem in their hordes, I would have believed that the Holy Land was crumbling, taking the entire corrupt world with it. The military was mobilized to set up dozens of tents for those without shelter, and emergency food distribution points were established throughout the city. Under Roman rule, Herod was likewise called 'to Order' following a similar phenomenon. Now, in 1927, it was our turn.

Scientists told us the earthquake was a natural catastrophe, affecting everyone regardless of religious or national affiliation, however it was evident that most victims were very poor, living in rickety homes or crumbling shelters. Since the British had arrived in Jerusalem, they had stationed their administrative headquarters in the Augusta Victoria building on Mount Scopus. After the earthquake, surveyors found the foundations of the building had cracked, and significant work was needed to repair them. This was an opportunity to implement my plans for a new and spacious government building. The area around Jebel Mukaber (the Great Mountain) provided more than 60dunams[3] of land, and it was decided that it would be the site of the new project.

When I say 'provided', I touch on another sensitive point – namely, allocation of land in the city –which calls for elaboration. Many of the city's lands, especially building plots, were owned by the major churches. At the end of the Russian Tsarist rule (not as far back as the nineteenth century, as some may think, but only a few years before I arrived in Jerusalem), the Orthodox Church's influence began to wane such that it was forced to rent or sell most of its properties. The area adjacent to Jaffa Street, for example, leased to the British police, maintained its name the 'Russian Compound', but preserved its Russian character in name only. Similarly, the new neighbourhoods of the city, and the new buildings to be erected, were nearly all on lands purchased from one of the churches. The land of Jebel Mukaber, designated for the government building, was no exception and was acquired near the new neighbourhood of Talpiot. All this brings us back to the sensitive issue of Zionism: many of the lands the Zionists acquired in Palestine came from the same source and were obtained under similar circumstances.

Five different plans and several years of budget debates and changes were required before the government building was finally complete. Although I can't recall every accusation levelled against me at the time, many accused me of being extravagant, claiming that what I lacked in physical stature I compensated for in the size of the building. When one governor demanded I incorporate into my drawings separate toilets for the English and non-English, the subsequent governor accused me of wastefulness or even discrimination. The animal cemetery that I planned for the Commissioner's House was also the subject of endless jokes, but I guess that's how things go.

In general, the issue of cemeteries in the city has been particularly sensitive and has caused quite a few controversies, hindering in the case of the museum the excavation for the building's foundations. Jerusalem was, and still is, surrounded by burial hills. The idea to build the museum in the northeast corner of the Old City wall was both excellent and problematic. Whilst there were interesting archaeological remnants on the chosen hill, implementing a construction site in the heart of a massive necropolis turned out to be quite a delicate feat. Hundreds of graves from the Roman and Byzantine periods were discovered during the digging, and as the one responsible for the project, I had to implore the gods that no Muslim or Jewish graves would be found later: it would have disrupted the entire construction process.

8

By this time, I had assembled around me a team of technical, archaeological and linguistic advisers who contributed significantly to advancing building plans for the museum. These men and women also enriched my working hours with their vital enthusiasm and complementary opinions. Holding back the entire process would have been disastrous for me, personally and professionally.

Hanan Nashashibi, for example, was the first modern Arab woman I got to know personally. Although we had more than good working relations, I cannot say that we became very close. The issues preventing this were more cultural than personal. She usually wore a traditional dress but with European high heels. Hanan wore makeup and liked modern perfume, but her behaviour code was very Eastern. She had extraordinary knowledge of the Semitic languages and, for instance, explained to me the geographical boundaries of Levantine Arabic. It was interesting to compare these boundaries with political borders, which were completely different: the mountains of Damascus to the north and the Negev desert and the city of al-Arish to the southwest. Palestinian Arabic, it turns out, succeeded in preserving a highly classical structure and retained in its spoken language many literary forms of expression. It is, nevertheless, a vibrant and lively tongue, sensitive to various historical influences and local nuances such as those of the Bedouins. I was surprised, for example, that the name Abu Tor –the neighbourhood where I lived – kept the Aramaic word for mountain *Tor*, and that the commonly used word for 'table' is based on the Latin word *tabula*.

Hanan was not exceptionally beautiful, but she had an exotic allure of her own. At times she completely lost me with her detailed explanations, which was more to do with my immaturity as a male than to the subject matter. Yet Hanan knew, at such times, how to bring me back to reality to take certain decisions, such as naming the museum's different exhibition halls, cloakroom or library in the three official languages. She had unique manners and always found a way to argue a point without hurting my feelings. She once said, however, that we English are too sensitive: "Even our local peppers need peeling for clients such as you", she would joke, "to prevent, as you claim, 'two days of stomach pain and vomiting'". And she knew what she was talking about, as my housekeeper's favourite recipe for a Shakshuka omelet included hot pepper sauce, which I couldn't handle. How did I suddenly start talking about food?

One spring day in 1927, when the fields were still green and dotted with red and black poppies, an extraordinary event interrupted the monotony of my work: the Graf Zeppelin arrived. Remember that airplanes were uncommon at that time, and so seeing an airship of this size in the sky was for many an entirely new phenomenon. Unfortunately, none of the vibrant colours of the day were evident in the black-and-white cardboard photo I received as a souvenir of the event. It's also a shame that the construction of the museum proceeded so slowly, as the photo shows only the laying of its foundations and the neatly stacked stone ready for construction. The hill was known as the vineyard of Sheikh Muhammad al-Khalili, and his summer house can be seen in the photo alongside the dressed stones and the lonely pine tree, all black with its needles.

The LZ 127 Graf Zeppelin flew gracefully over Jerusalem, illustrating how air routes now connected Asia and Europe with the United States and the rest of the world. Indeed, it brought to places such as London and Athens mail that had been delayed for months. This brings us back to my own building projects, because I was the one who planned and built the two most important Palestinian post offices of that period – in Jaffa and in Jerusalem – to which such mail was delivered.

9

If I had difficulty getting close to Hanan, it was different with Omar, the Palestinian archaeologist for the museum project; we had a direct and friendly connection. More than once, we found ourselves sitting together for lunch, each drawing food out of the bag he brought. Usually, it was on Sheikh's Hill, where excavation had begun, but sometimes on the city wall near Herod's Gate or even in the courtyard of one of Omar's friend's homes in the Bab al-Sharqiya neighbourhood. Omar came from a large family and was the fourth of six children, two of whom passed away at a young age. His father and uncle sold fruit and vegetables and occasionally negotiated the sale of agricultural plots. I remember they were careful not to sell land, directly or indirectly, to the Jewish Agency or to anyone associated with Zionism. Awareness of the deepening rift between sides slowly seeped into all layers of the population. The contradictory British promises to both the Arabs and the Jews caused growing frustration and, worse, resentment. Most of the lands that were not church lands were registered in the names of wealthy owners residing in Cairo or Damascus who were less scrupulous about the affiliation or identity of potential buyers. However, no local landowners would dream of selling to a Jewish buyer.

Some people, like Orde, viewed such a stance as extreme, and considered me not just backward but quite literally reactionary."You are a Jew hater of the most outmoded kind", he told me when we met at the opening night of the King David Hotel. "You refuse to see that between 'the new settlers' and the Jewish rag-and-bone peddlers from the fourteenth century, there isn't the slightest connection. Someone like Moshe Dayan is a soldier in the tradition of the Maccabees. Just like them, members of the Hagannah will rebuild the Temple in Jerusalem. Someone like you should be open and aware of the moves of history."

"The Temple of today", I replied, "should be universal, not bloody nationalistic."

He sniggered and wiped away some spittle from his lips. "As I've already said, you're an antiquated romantic. Your archaeological temple, if ever built, will stand empty and haunting in its solitude. Look at the Wailing Wall, for example, all black, dusty and dilapidated. Your museum will be as sacred and majestic, just like it."

"The bankers and arms dealers you meet right and left will only lead you downwards," I replied, "and the eternal holy book that you always carry with you won't be of much help."

"Let's meet in another ten or twenty years", he said, unaware that he wouldn't survive that long. According to hearsay, he rejected the opinions of meteorologists and insisted on flying in very dangerous conditions. As I've mentioned, his is the tragic story of Lawrence revisited, just in its Hebrew version: T. E. Lawrence also ended his life in an absurd motorcycle accident that had no logical explanation.

If I sound a bit negative about the years I spent in Jerusalem, let me tell you about David Ohannessian.[4] That will change the tone of my story. When I'm told sometimes that there is no bad without good, I think straightaway of Mark Sykes. I know it seems like I'm digressing again, but it will become clear soon why I mention him. Sykes represented Britain in a negotiated contract known since then by its name, the Sykes–Picot Agreement. Picot was the French diplomat with whom the British had outlined the problematic division of the Middle East we inherited, Palestine being part of it. He naturally supported the Balfour Declaration, and it's clear to me that Mark Sykes represents the twisted element of British presence in that part of the world. But what is the good point in all this? Sykes was responsible for bringing David – or 'Dvot' in Armenian – to Jerusalem.

David was born in Turkey to an Armenian family. Although his father passed away when he was still young and he had to start work when he was still a child, he became a very successful ceramicist. As a young man he was invited to renovate, for example, tiles in the Holy City of Mecca. With the beginning of the massacre of Armenians in Turkey, David fled and settled in the Syrian city of Aleppo. He lost most of his family in the riots. But when Sykes met him in Syria, he invited him to restore and renovate tiles in the Holy City of Jerusalem. Incidentally, the workshop he opened was called The Tiles of the Dome of the Rock. There wasn't a more talented potter than David, and when it came to the design and execution of all the ceramic works in the museum – from the pools to the fountains and floor tiles –no one else could have achieved such masterful work. Even on a non-professional level, there isn't a single negative thing to say about him. David was an exemplary family man, but his age and social circles were so different from mine that I didn't see much of him outside working hours.

10

Anna Badurian was also part of the same group of dedicated people that formed around the establishment of the museum. She became David's personal assistant, as her work at the Armenian clinic did not provide her with an income. Anna came to Jerusalem during the wave of migration from Turkey and Syria, dedicating herself to orphans and other persons in distress. After the earthquake there was even more work for her, but as I mentioned, she couldn't sustain herself without a salary.

In those days, much was said about Jewish and Arab immigration but few mentioned the thousands of Armenian migrants. Jews hardly differentiated between Armenians and Arabs, and similarly, for Palestinians, they seemed like European Christians. Although the old-time Armenians of Jerusalem spoke Arabic and adopted many local customs, those who migrated during the Turkish massacres were quite different and struggled to adapt to the Middle Eastern atmosphere of the city. Anna was much more Western than the local Armenians, and in my eyes, was a perfect blend of East and West. She was truly beautiful.

11

One Saturday, I met Hanan by the Sa'id brothers' bookstore, at the entrance to the Old City. I liked buying ground coffee or dried tea from the spice vendors in the traditional market, enjoying all the aromas and colours. In a humorous tone I said to Hanan, "I'm already looking forward to receiving a wedding invitation."

"This is not a joking matter. You know, my fiancé, Ali, belongs to the so-called Husseini tribe."

"I'm not very well versed in the intricacies of local family relationships", I replied. "I only know that Husseini has gained power recently in local politics."

"Exactly, and his family isn't particularly fond of the families of the Khalidis or the Nashashibis, meaning me. We had no choice but to separate."

"I'm sorry", I said.

"I hope that in the future, we'll have more honourable leaders", she replied.

"Look," I said, "even an intelligent politician such as Weizmann is currently side-lined."

"I don't like comparing *Khalal* to *Haram*," Hanan said, "but you're right; all the moderates are being pushed slowly into a corner. The moment I have a professional opportunity, I'm thinking of leaving this provincial city."

"Provincial?" I pointed to the bookstore. "In which nearby city will you find such a book store? In Amman? In Damascus?"

"And how many such bookstores are there in Jerusalem? Exactly one. And how many cinemas? Exactly one. And how many beauty salons are there for women?"

"I know what you mean," I replied, "but the city is changing, albeit slowly. In any case, you're not allowed to leave before the museum opens."

"I promise", she said, not knowing that neither of us would be present on that auspicious day. We worked together for many years, but Hanan would be killed in the riots of 1936, and I left Jerusalem a short whilst later in disgust. But I'm getting way ahead of myself.

I worked on the museum plans for more than four years, and another eight years passed before its construction was complete. Its final inauguration had to wait for an additional two years, mainly due to the tense political situation. A few hours before the official opening commenced, one of the responsible archaeologists, Starky, was brutally murdered. Of course, I couldn't foretell all these complications when I started working on the project, so I'll do my best to recount the stages of its birth, chapter by chapter.

12

I knew that the quality of the building should be evident both in its overall design and in its details, and that's why I insisted on bringing Eric Gill, the English craftsman,[5] to Jerusalem. Gill was supposed to design and carve all the stone reliefs and stone signage. As early as 1930, both David and Eric had received the various measurements and precise location of each item they were supposed to create, and they worked on them until 1933.

In some respects, Gill was the left-wing counterpart to Wingate. He had the same romantic and messianic character, only leaning towards the Oriental rather than the Jewish. When he came to Jerusalem, he walked around in full Arab garb, and in this regard, at least, he had a certain advantage over Orde, who was often seen stark naked. But in other respects, he was much worse, especially sexually. According to his own testimony, no dog or goat in Jerusalem at that time was safe from his advances. Personally, I was much more concerned about the young Bedouin girls who lived near the construction site of the museum. It turned out that even Gill's own daughters were victims of his sexual proclivities.

However, Gill was a first-rate artist. Without a doubt, the museum owed much of its international reputation to his sculptures and bas-reliefs. Gill was also an extraordinary letter-cutter, and he redesigned the entire alphabet for the museum's signage – Arabic, Hebrew and English. Thanks to craftsmen like him, the museum was slowly becoming a cornerstone of internationalism. Gill belonged to a revolutionary English artists' movement that made a name for itself mainly in the field of design. I say 'artists' movement' and not 'art movement' because the people involved were very different from one another. Artists created their own style rather than strive for a common, single genre. What bound them together was their rediscovery of pre-industrial craftsmanship. They wanted to explore and revive handicrafts for the twentieth century. This heritage included the stone carvings of the Middle Ages and the text inscriptions on stone, two domains in which Gill became an expert.

He was also highly religious and worked with many churches back in England. Don't ask me how all this fits with his other character traits mentioned earlier; if there's one thing I've learnt over the years, it's that we are all made up of various components. There is no good without bad, and no bad without good.

13

On my way home one day, I saw Ofra waiting for someone in front of the train station. The railway tracks had been repaired and the trains were running on time. I didn't mention that my home was located close to the station and that the whole square in front of it was, for me, an irresistible arena for observation and wonderment. It's difficult, perhaps, to imagine nowadays that a small station like the one next to Abu Tor attracted such a broad spectrum of human beings from around the world: pilgrims, arms smugglers, politicians... the lot. Not to mention immigrants, legal or illegal, from places such as Moscow, Paris or Madrid. I seized the opportunity to get information from Ofra about the Jewish organizations in Palestine.

"Why do you hate the Arabs so much?" I asked her.

"We don't", she answered doggedly.

"But you disparage them."

"We just don't know them", Ofra explained.

"You study every trail and valley around the city, but you don't bother to get to know the simple residents here."

"Look, Mr Austin," she said, "you are perhaps an exception, but how many of you British know Arabs? You might know the millionaires that throw banquets for you, but the simple residents, Arab or Jewish, don't interest you at all."

"And your neighbours", I asked, "here in Abu Tor, don't you make an effort to get to know them?"

"You, more than me, ought to be familiar with the English saying: 'A man's home is his castle.'"

I mumbled something about how interesting Arabic is as a language and how close it is to Hebrew. Then two of Ofra's friends arrived, and they left me as if leaving a bicycle. It was clear I wouldn't get very far with Ofra.

14

Omar, our archaeologist, and Anna the Armenian had meanwhile become a couple. I can't say that I accepted it very well. Without thinking about it much, I had probably developed some expectations about Anna and me, so, initially, I took it to heart. When I say 'initially', I mean for the first year or so of their relationship. Later, I'm happy to say, they became my closest friends in Jerusalem.

As I mentioned in the context of David Ohannessian, Anna was also an Armenian from Anatolia, but unlike David, she came directly from Europe. She could barely speak Arabic and was mostly in contact with the local Armenians. Her English wasn't bad, and it amused me that it became the language, along with some Turkish, that she and Omar used to communicate. Despite Anna's tragic past – she was born in Anatolia during the genocide–she was full of life, and her dimples added an irresistible charm. She always had something positive to say about someone, or a smile to spare, yet she was far from being naïve. Although she didn't want me to say a word about it to Omar, she told me she carried two knives in the folds of her skirt in case someone tried to harm her. "If I have to leave the world," she told me, "I'm taking the murderer with me, and perhaps one or two of his friends at the same time." More than anything else, she was afraid of being a passive victim, like so many of her family back in Turkey. Anna radiated such vitality that it was indeed hard to imagine an end to her life, except perhaps in self-defence. Omar was much less exuberant and talkative but no less amusing and lively. He looked at everything as if the smallest of details mattered to him, a bit like when he examined a rare archaeological item.

I must admit with some embarrassment that, for months, I kept close track of Anna and Omar's relationship. To witness a young couple openly exchange tender looks and unashamedly brush against each other, was something new to me. Back in the United Kingdom, courting comprised endless rituals of opening car doors, writing romantic letters and the gentleman-like removal of a woman's coat. But could courting be done differently? I watched them closely whilst respecting their space, trying to avoid posing overly intimate questions. They found my curiosity amusing, but nothing could prevent them from being close. The simplicity of Anna and Omar amazed me. The closest parallel I could find to their particular relationship was in Shakespeare's writing, but even there the directness was poetic and the simplicity contrived compared to what I saw in my friends' relationship. Clearly, I wanted to know what the making of such a union consisted of.

Looking up from my museum drawings, I reflected on my attitude to the United States. I found that Americans may have the charm and enthusiasm that young children sometimes have, traits which surprisingly endeared them to me. Due to the common language and related historical developments, one tends to view the United States as a younger sister to Great Britain, but as happens in the best of families, fraternal relationships may be fraught with tension. The power that the United States has accumulated, and continues to accumulate, in the world, terrifies me to the depths of my soul. Sticking with the nursery analogy, one could liken the United States to an infant armed with a semi-automatic rifle; whenever he feels like it, or he gets scared or disappointed or is tickled excessively, he could kill countless people...

The tremendous sums that the Americans made available and our own government's increasing dependence on America drove me out of my wits sometimes. The fact the construction of the YMCA building, for example, progressed so much faster than that of our government building and the museum struck us like ... like bum notes sung during church choir practice. Whilst we had to settle for limited budgets, content ourselves with a Jewish contractor named Shapira and a third-rate Italian construction company, American engineers found all sorts of shortcuts to complete their building project ahead of us. Not only that, but Harmon their architect had to elevate the building higher than any other structure in the city. This was for him not that challenging, given he had been involved in planning New York's tallest skyscraper, the Empire State. Later, for the inauguration of the YMCA, the Americans invited more famous people to the grand and bombastic ceremony – befitting an American project – than the British managed to invite to the inauguration of the Commissioner's House. Today, both buildings stand on opposite sides of Old Jerusalem, from the west and south-east of the city, bearing silent witnesses to what I'm talking about.

Through Omar and many of the English archaeologists, I learnt about the illegal trade in antiquities: about a third of the local archaeological finds disappeared almost as soon as they had been discovered. It was easy to blame the Bedouin or Arab workers whose meagre wages barely covered their most basic needs when in fact much more sophisticated and cunning intermediaries – Arab Christians, Armenians or Jews – were responsible for most of the illicit trade in antiquities. The Muslim Arabs were too naïve at the time to develop a proper escape route for their loot. When a Hebrew or Aramaic inscription was discovered during the excavations, we had to immediately hire an armed guard to protect the find until a safer place could be found for it. American traders began to roam the excavation area and buy anything they could get their hands on, provided it was even remotely related to the Holy Scriptures. Within the first month of digging, two incidents raised our awareness of the problem.

Incidentally, it must be said that if the incidents hadn't, sadly, involved robbery, they would have been comical.

In an immense garage in the Sheikh Jarrah neighbourhood, a British driver looking for spare parts discovered that the garage not only repaired European cars but also housed stolen parts from such cars, and even included a museum with about twenty stolen Morgans, Bentleys and the most recent Austins. In addition, there was a structure next to the garage containing objects from every possible historical period, all for sale of course. Our police acted immediately, but in many cases it was already too late. It was impossible to know from which archaeological site and exact location all those items had been removed.

The second event was even more absurd. On this occasion, an American tourist was also invited to the Salameh Villa in Talbiya, where I was a guest from time to time, for an evening meal. Proudly, unashamedly, she showed me an ancient stone bead necklace displayed on her half-exposed chest. The same necklace had been in the hands of Omar just two weeks earlier following the discovery of an ancient burial cave in the Sheikh Abu Khalil field. When we learnt that the American guest was staying in one of the consulate houses and that the cleaner of that house was the wife of one of the guards we had hired, the solution to the mystery of how she came to be in possession of the necklace was revealed. On that evening, I mentioned only the facts and did not insist that she return the necklace, but a day or two later an Armenian merchant came and offered us the very item for a modest sum. We paid the man to avoid a scandal, but the whole affair left a bitter taste in the mouth. The guard involved had to find a new job, of course.

As well as the British, Palestinian residents and occasionally the Americans also organized social events, and they were often boisterous and cosmopolitan affairs. One of the prominent figures amongst the American personalities was Clinton Hart. Whether in Jerusalem or at his villa in Tiberias, the evenings at his residences required neither formal invitation nor an announcement in the classifieds; the loud conversations and the unrestrained laughter of his guests were enough to inform passers-by that an event was on. Dozens gathered, mindless of official attire or other societal conventions, reminding us Brits that our standing in the world was gradually diminishing. Perhaps it was excessive sensitivity on my part, but I found the growing influence of this empire beyond the Atlantic Ocean alarming, legitimized solely on account of its economy and technology.

It was at the Salameh family villa that I met the famous Arab singer Fatima. I won't divulge her real name because at that time she was still a teenager, and even now I hesitate to recount details of that evening. Nevertheless, suffice to say that the young Diva shattered within a few short minutes the image I had had of her prior to our meeting.

On the pretext of looking for a light for her cigarette, which she held in her hand, and despite my apology that I didn't smoke, Fatima reached into the pocket of my slacks. We were standing in a corner of the living room at that moment, where no one noticed us. But, instead of a lighter, she retrieved from my pocket a tiny silver penknife, which I usually carried with me. According to her, it was a souvenir she must keep by which to 'remember' me. *Remember* me?

"But we don't know each other at all!" I exclaimed.

"That's what you say", the singer said drunkenly, pushing me into the corridor. Then, with a strength I didn't expect from a 17-year-old, she forced her lipstick-coated lips onto mine. This was perhaps my first adult kiss, if one may refer to the unreciprocated pressing of one's mouth onto another's as a 'kiss'.

I mumbled an apology, even though I had nothing to apologize for, left the girl a 10s note and, once I had recovered my penknife from the floor and washed traces of lipstick from my face in the restrooms, made my way to the exit. Asking why I was leaving early, my hosts assured me that such incidents with Fatima were quite common and that she was in constant search of dosh. It took me a while to find my words and thank them for the evening. I put on my overcoat and stepped outside, not knowing what to make of the incident.

15

The narrative may give the impression that I drifted from one evening meal to another, but the truth is that I lived modestly, almost like a monk. If I recall this event or another, it's because it was so different from the other evenings I spent in the city. I had in my room a simple wooden bed, a table, a chair and a small shelf with all my belongings and a few books to which I returned again and again. My clothes hung on a simple wooden rod. I refused to be driven in one of the British cars offered to me unless it was for a formal meeting at a distant location.

Occasionally, I was called to meetings in Damascus or Cairo, but I travelled to those by train. As I mentioned, I got to most of my sites in Jerusalem on foot or occasionally by horse and cart. There were no cars in Abu Tor and very few horses. Donkeys ruled the neighbourhood, and the sound of their braying, along with the crowing of the roosters, woke me up early in the morning. I found them more endearing than the calls to prayer from the nearby mosque that sometimes woke me up as well, but at a much less reasonable hour. I discovered that the combination of Arab and Christian elements was much closer to my personal temperament.

Just to complete the picture I've painted of my life in Jerusalem in those days, I should mention that I gradually adapted to local customs. For example, I usually had breakfast and lunch at home unless I had planned a long day of work outdoors. On those occasions, Ayuna, the cook, prepared bread rolls, hard-boiled eggs, some tahini, parsley and coriander for me, and sometimes even raw garlic and fresh onions that I learnt to eat 'like a big boy'. However, I couldn't tolerate the local *skhug*, a specialty paste made with green chilli peppers and other chopped roots and herbs: everyone has their limitations.

I remember that Ayuna prepared an exceptional breakfast on my thirty-sixth birthday: *fatayer* pastries soaked in rosewater. With my morning tea, it was a real treat. She also refused to give me the usual hard-boiled egg for lunch and instead handed me a small pot of lamb and lentil stew, which I particularly liked. Of course, I had no choice but to call upon the services of a stubborn donkey to take me to the museum site where, come noon time, I reheated the stew on a primus stove. Interestingly, the cornerstone for the museum was laid that same week, so you could say our birthdays coincided.

Other birthdays were entirely solitary celebrations for me, not to mention weekends when I hardly saw anyone. I avoided the city centre or the area between the walls from Friday to Sunday because a kind of tribal, religious frenzy prevailed there. Entire families descended on market stalls, stocking up on food and other supplies as if preparing for a siege. Others hurried to the bathhouse before visiting the mosque or synagogue. The Apocalypse, it seemed, was announced by the clanging of church bells that echoed from every corner, and the muezzin called out in confirmation, as if for the Day of Judgement. The ultra-Orthodox of the three religions roamed the streets like ghosts, and the murmuring of prayers sounded no less alarming to me than the bells. Nevertheless, I felt strongly that Jerusalem was where I belonged; almost as Kafka knew he had no other life but that of *The Trial*, or the insect-like existence he described in *The Metamorphosis*.

However, it slowly dawned on me that I might remain single forever. Not just because there weren't enough opportunities to meet women with whom I would be happy to share my life, but because I felt a certain lack of confidence, almost physical, closely tied to the geographical, political or cultural isolation I've just described. It seemed that the ship of my life needed to finally berth in some safe haven, yet I had no idea when and where it might be. In any case, uncertainty was in the air and, over the years, it only intensified. For me, these were emblematic inter-world war years. Jerusalem was a city of refugees and fervent religious zealots. What exactly was I doing there?

I wandered the city for hours, discovering each time a different part, such as the Templar residences in the German Quarter which, despite the sweet scent of pine in the air, inspired a sort of seriousness that I didn't particularly welcome. I would bypass the Quarter's former leper house and return to Abu Tor through the open olive groves.

Another day, I would walk in the direction of Hebron until I reached the square houses of the new Talpiot. Here, plump European cats feasted on European leftovers, attempting to bestow on the neighbourhood a hominess that it still lacked. It had been built as a 'Bauhaus' neighbourhood, but the new industrial stucco finish of the walls repelled me.

In the Montefiore neighbourhood, the scents were of Balkan or Yemeni food that I couldn't quite identify, and the cats were much leaner. Elderly women in colourful attire washed the stone stairs with soapy water, scrubbing them with a short, straw broom. Sometimes I would descend towards the Old City, raising dust with my English brogues as I followed the donkey trails. Dodging the small stone houses, I would inhale the aroma of burning dung and the appetizing smell of fresh pita bread. I was a foreign refugee in a biblical landscape, an eternal tectonic plate that had survived occupation by countless cultures.

The museum was supposed to encompass all those cultures that Jerusalem had survived or, to be more positive, to present the changing identities of the city throughout the generations. Instead of 'changing', one could also say 'accumulating', but I don't particularly like that word. Perhaps 'adding' best describes the schizophrenia of the Holy City. How many of you have heard of 'Jerusalem Syndrome'? I digress, but the fact that so many foreigners living in the city lose their minds, for a while at least, reflects my fifteen years' experience there.

I heard about dozens of pilgrims, and I even saw quite a few, who were convinced upon arriving in the city that the Holy Spirit had descended upon them, and from then on they embodied the renewed birth of this or that prophet. I'm not convinced that Lawrence and Wingate didn't belong in a similar category. There was something about the collective schizophrenia of Jerusalem that triggered in certain visitors a previously dormant personality disorder. Such visitors would position themselves on street corners, entreating the crowd to amend their ways before it was too late or prepare for the coming of the Messiah. Some wished to cleanse the Holy City of all infidels before the ultimate day, and others heard voices or claimed that some specific task had been imposed on them. My task was the museum.

As I sit down to write, preparing to elaborate on the planning of the museum, I find myself lost for the appropriate words. In fact, I didn't feel that any Holy Spirit had descended upon me, and I think that despite my personal frustrations, I managed to maintain a certain mental equilibrium. Nevertheless, there was a sense of mission to my work. I was a servant of the British Empire, with a hereditary, national and universal obligation to incarnate the mandate Britain received for Palestine. If nothing else, I had a commitment to build something of lasting importance. I had a recurring dream then, which sometimes involved a deserted megalithic structure in an English forest or an observation tower in Anatolia. Almost always, the structure had an octagonal form with an aura around it, like that of a precious and glittering stone. On other occasions, it reminded me of a lighthouse or an ancient temple.

I wanted to build such a structure, but intended it to be modern or even utopian. Of course, I didn't mention this vision to anyone, and there was no need to. For me, what counted was that the museum would exist. Once constructed, I could disappear, be assassinated by an extremist Jew or Arab, be sent to India or back to England, become a mundane and boring family man or remain single, but the museum had to be established.

I made dozens, perhaps hundreds, of drawings for the museum at every possible hour of the day or night. Eventually, I condensed these drawings into one, representative plan. Looking at it today, the plan seems a bit too rigid to me in its severe symmetry, lacking somewhat the spontaneous, haphazard look of typical Arab villages that I used as a model. Perhaps the chaotic political atmosphere of those days explains my need for security through geometric, abstract forms. Evidently, I was in search of peace and could find it only within the protected walls of a monastery, away from the turbulent world outside.

16

Had these present pages been fiction and not a summary of my fifteen years stay in Jerusalem, one could have read the following chapter as a detective story. It would then have the gruesome title 'The Black Hand against the White Book'. However, this isn't the time or place for flippancy. The 1930s and 40s in Jerusalem were consecutive decades of bloodshed, following which the British government was forced to abandon its mandate and return home. The Black Hand, led by Sheikh Izz ad-Din al-Qassam, was an Arab terrorist organization established in 1930 that aimed to disrupt Jewish immigration and acquisition of land in Palestine. It's worth noting that, during those same years, the Nazis rose to power in Germany, prompting many Jewish residents to flee Europe, notably towards the land of Israel. Alongside the Jewish defense organization, terrorist groups like Etzel and Lehi were also formed. Hundreds of men, women and children paid with their lives as a result of all these terrorist activities. Such events delayed establishment of the museum at various stages and disrupted the supply of materials more than once. I could feel the situation worsening from week to week. Personally, for fear of being attacked, I kept a low profile and was cautious when choosing which paths to use.

At one point, the Jewish residents of Talpiot were asked to evacuate their homes because of the tense situation. The proximity of the neighbourhood to multiple Arab settlements made the British stationed in the nearby Allenby Camp uneasy; blame for any incidents involving Jews would automatically be directed at them. The Government House itself was just a short walk from Talpiot. The Hebrew writer Agnon's response to the evacuation was: "There was no reason for me to leave the ghetto in Poland. Once again, we are in a ghetto-like position, Jews surrounded by the heathen." And speaking of Talpiot, the German-Jewish architect Kauffmann was originally responsible for its creation. Fortunately for its inhabitants, the Jewish-English architect Benjamin Chaikin joined him, adding over time more sympathetic roofs and awnings to the original stark, functional German cubes.

One evening during that time, I was surprised to hear a knock on my door. It was Ofra, who did not wish to enter but came to seek my help in releasing her friends from detention. I told her hesitantly that I was not acquainted with the British police officers here in Jerusalem, although that wasn't entirely accurate. I was, to put it cautiously, sympathetic towards the Arabs, who criticized the massive immigration of Jews from Europe, yet it wasn't individual pilgrims praying by the Western Wall of the Temple or some passers-by wearing a skullcap who were responsible for this massive immigration, so self-defence groups were clearly justified.

From my perspective, rather than killing innocent residents, it would have been better for the undercover groups to target our own military posts, as those responsible for the present situation were, in fact, the British. Had they refrained from bluntly dividing the Turkish loot between themselves and the French, everything in the Middle East would have looked different. The Jewish insurgency seemed dangerous to me all the same, and I knew it would inevitably lead to full-scale warfare. Ofra's parents, or any of the Jewish immigrants, had to prevent their children from taking part in such dangerous activities. After all, Ofra was just a young girl, perhaps 21 or 22 years old at the most.

At weekends, she and her friends looked so beautiful when they removed the ridiculous khaki and dressed in clothes suitable for their age. I saw them sometimes heading towards Bethlehem, visiting Rachel's Tomb, if I'm not mistaken, or to one of the springs around the city, or just sitting on some wall, peeling cucumbers or merrily munching a tomato. It seemed to me that they had even fewer inhibitions than people like Omar and Anna, but I also found that without a spiritual framework or universal goals, their sensuality could lead only to frustration and violence. In any case, I thought I should at least ask Edward Keith about the arrests. That would give me, if nothing else, an excuse to knock on Ofra's parents' door. Until then, I had been invited only to the homes of Palestinians, never to Jewish homes.

17

In 1921, Winston Churchill, in all his glory, visited Jerusalem. Suddenly, amongst the horses and carts, camels and donkey riders, luxurious limousines could be seen on the city streets. Most of the roads were, of course, not suitable for such vehicles, but that was one of the reasons why the British were in Jerusalem: to build roads, that is. In my opinion, T.E. Lawrence was largely responsible for persuading Churchill to come. Churchill tended to belittle Palestine as a colony, attaching much greater importance to India or even Sudan and Egypt. He didn't have, how to say, the sensitivity of Lawrence or even Wingate to everything related to the Middle East. For him, Palestine was just a strategic point between Africa and Asia and, potentially, a solution to the Jewish problem in Europe. Churchill stuttered like a child on occasion such that, at times, it was hard for me to acknowledge that he was the British Secretary of State for the Colonies.

Typically, it was not in the Commissioner's House but in the King David Hotel where I finally had a conversation with Churchill. The

Minister of Settlements of Britain stayed there for a few days, and seemed to be busy, continuously, with eating and smoking. I understood only a percentage of what he said, but our conversation went something like this:

"Without the Jewish settlement program, Palestine will look like the rest of the Middle East: desert and camel caravans", Churchill declared.

"There's no shortage of camels, even in Jerusalem. Haven't you seen the horse and camel stables at the back of the hotel?" I asked.

"I've seen, I've seen. But I also saw the Buicks and Fords parked there."

"It's not the Buicks and Fords that will save Jerusalem."

"Look, my dear Austen, it seems to me that you live in a somewhat poetic world. The Jewish economy also sustains building projects like the ones you're involved with."

"Sir Churchill, can you imagine a solution in Palestine that will not be followed by endless bloodshed? With the current Jewish immigration, demographic figures will soon balance here, leading eventually to a Jewish majority."

"Look," said Churchill, "Weizmann already meets with Abdullah. Ben-Gurion prepares a deal with the Mufti, negotiated by Al-Alami. If we can encourage further meetings of this kind, diplomacy will win where rifles fail."

"I'm very pessimistic", I warned."My feeling is that we're losing control of the situation."

I left the hotel late that evening. A few years later, in the very same hall where I had sat with Churchill, dozens of people would lose their lives, including some high-ranking British officers. A Jewish terror organization sent its agents to teach us a lesson in 'sabotage' and 'revolutionary propaganda'. In a separate incident, Churchill's close friend Lord Moyne and his chauffeur found themselves the target of Jewish bullets.

18

Were these evenings the equivalent of the *Titanic*'s ballroom dances, just before it sank? Many of our army officers and government officials were capable of moving on from a reception in the Commissioner's House to an American party in the YMCA, ending their night in Sheikh Jarrah in the company of the Antonius couple and their friends. I had hoped that the main hall of the government residence would be used for cultural events such as concerts or lectures. Rather, I found that, instead of coming to Jerusalem, someone such as the conductor Arturo Toscanini favoured the industrial spaces of Tel Aviv's Yarid Hamizrakh exhibition halls for his concerts, together with his Jewish musician friends. Indeed, I had encountered a world turned upside down.

Like a mythical battle where forces of darkness fight against light, or light against darkness, I fought for the establishment of the museum. The funding for the construction of the museum was, ultimately, an affair that not only embarrassed the British Commissioner but also cast a certain shadow over its very existence. One of the richest families in the world, if not the richest – the Rockefellers – covered some of the construction and initial operation costs of the museum. As one might guess, the Rockefellers are American. I wouldn't be surprised if one day the museum bears their name, but I hope by then that I will have removed myself from this cursed place.

No one wanted to listen to my criticism. I began to hear comments like 'Why is the architect interfering all of a sudden?' or 'Which mosquito bit Austen?' By nature I was not a political person, but as a British subject, shame gradually took hold of me until I felt suffocated. In hindsight, it seemed that most officials were happy to get rid of me, not only because of the protest I expressed regarding the government's stance in the local political conflict, but also because they found that 'my taste in building became too expensive for them. I was just keen to see my building projects through to a satisfactory stage before handing in my notice.

19

The Middle East, which I once envisioned as a vast ocean of sand, barren granite mountains and winsome flocks of bell-carrying sheep, suddenly became small and constricted, like a segregated ethnic quarter. Instead of supporting a solid and modern Middle Eastern kingdom, the new Englishmen doodled arbitrary maps every few months, signed agreements and communicated with dubious, temporary allies. A new White Paper was published with each change of the season, yet there was never a clear and principled policy. In my daily life, the results were manifest in terrorist activities. From 1929 onwards, but especially after 1936, violence became almost routine. The interruption or lack of building supplies, the absence of skilled workers and sporadic killings all contributed to the deterioration of my professional situation. It was only a matter of time, it seemed, before war would break out.

Death penalties were declared for all unauthorised weapon holders. Jerusalem became an enclosed detention camp – a kind of enlarged Russian Compound where everyone was considered suspicious – and British torture methods achieved notoriety. I could no longer bear to reside there, and it certainly held no spiritual aspirations for me.

I remember that the *Daily Mail* of that period enthusiastically announced that the British fascist organisation the Black Shirts was gaining strength and its youth movement was gaining popularity. It seemed that many women in England supported this political revival as well, and someone like Mary Richardson, who was previously known as a suffragette campaigner, became a national hero as Chief Organiser of the movement. It seemed to me that the nationalistic orientation that I had witnessed in Palestine was also raising its ugly head elsewhere around the world.

I knew that a significant and satisfactory period in my life was coming to an end, and I had to look for new options in a different British settlement. I wondered where there might be a sane place for me. Every day I read in the newspapers or heard accounts on the radio of tension, threat and confrontation around the globe. The time to go and find that haven of sanity, I realised, was now; not even the official opening ceremony of the museum could make me stay. 'Let them inaugurate the museum themselves,' I said to myself, 'and let them choke'. I joined two British cars bound for Egypt. Feeling at the same time a traitor and the one betrayed, I barely said goodbye to the many people I knew. My last pay cheque had to be expedited to Cairo.

20

As I might have mentioned, Fathy, the Egyptian architect, welcomed me in Cairo as if I were his older brother. His yellow leather slippers and brown robe awaited me at the entrance to his house, and behind him stood a rather bemused Dimitri Papadimos, his very young protégé. From the start, I felt paternal emotions towards Dimitri, and with satisfaction I noticed that he reciprocated the sentiment. From that moment onwards, ours was a kindred relationship. Despite much travelling on both sides, there wasn't a week when we didn't see or hear from each other, and this situation continues to this day. When he got married and settled in Athens after the war, I joined him and his wife as a kind of stepfather.

This raises an issue I find perplexing. With most people, I found that establishing a connection is difficult, and maintaining that connection is even more challenging. Did God, in his unfathomable and inaccessible wisdom, create and then scatter kin individuals around the globe whose task it would ultimately be to locate each other in the course of their lives? With Dimitri, we discovered this or that oasis in the golden deserts of Egypt, or island-hopped across the Mediterranean Sea on Greek tourist ships. Years later, with Dimitri and his wife, we renovated and furnished abandoned houses in Greece. Moments like these solidified our bond until there were very few doubts or questions remaining.

It's worth mentioning, perhaps, that Greece was quite a fascinating place to be during the war. For entire periods, one could imagine that the war hardly existed at all, and only towards the end did it become truly horrific and blood-soaked. But I'm getting ahead of my narrative.

21

Like Supreme Justice Storrs, I too moved from Palestine and Egypt to Cyprus. And, like him, I found that "there is no ascent in rank" after a city like Jerusalem. I couldn't bear the thought of returning to England, and staying in Cyprus or Greece seemed like a reasonable compromise: neither were as exotic as Asia or Africa, but at least they were more Middle Eastern than European. However, what I didn't appreciate at first was the intense rivalry between Greeks and Turks on Cyprus, a rivalry that later reminded me of what I had left behind in Jerusalem. Only this time, it was the Turks who opposed the Greek–English dominance.

I felt that, with fascism in Europe and capitalism on the other side of the Atlantic, Britain's global standing was in decline. Not very bright people were at its head, the nation resembling a group of travellers led by lame and blind guides. I loved and hated this Britain in equal measure. I hated it being dwarfed by fascism and capitalism, a near submission that could only end with the adoption of one or the other. I loved what once represented and could continue to represent England: its universities, its castles and manors, its yellow-green fields with sheep and wild ponies, and its gardens, cultivated and wild at the same time. Also, its people, who were modest but dignified, polite without exception; fellow countrymen with 'integrity' and a certain self-respect.

An English archaeologist I knew in the 1920s, Alfred Watkins, noticed that a straight line – which he called the Michael Line – linked the southwest of England to the city of Jerusalem. This line connected five different churches, all dedicated to the Archangel Michael.

Interestingly, I found myself living my adult life along this line. In fact, despite being dedicated to Saint Michael and not the Saint Barb of my middle name, I find myself in old age still on this same axis, in Athens.

Epilogue

Jerusalem was the most significant chapter of my work. There, my ideas solidified, and my perspective on the world took shape. Despite our optimism and ambition for the 'beginning of the new century', with the desire for renewal, change and distance from the past, the early years of the twentieth century were, in my view, overshadowed by the events of the late nineteenth century. Nationalism, violence, militarization and superfluous industrialization only intensified. Change, in my opinion, took place only after a cul-de-sac had been reached – a point of no return – meaning the nuclear bombing in Japan and the death camps in Germany. These past twenty years, since the end of World War II to the present day, represent for me the new era, or the real beginning of the twentieth century.

But is the contemporary world so different from the world that preceded it? It pains me that the world isn't much closer, not even slightly, to my ideals and of those close to me. Although I failed to continue the momentum of construction and the projects I worked on after the war, I'm not bitter. I only feel that I paid a price for the independence of my ideas, which either opposed the mainstream view or perhaps belonged to a past epoch. Personally, I regret the lack of stability and connection to a specific geography in my adult life – elements so crucial for building a family. Although my life since leaving Jerusalem has been beautiful, I always felt somewhat detached, more of an observer than a participant in the family developments of my friends. Above all, it was Liana and Dimitri Papadimos, and their son and grandchildren, who represented a surrogate family for me.

I look at the four tiles that I carry with me from one residence to another, which were not needed in the museum, and examine every detail that David Ohannessian crafted with love. The blues and greens inevitably bring the aquatic or celestial to mind; in water, as in the sky, we find the same free-floating layers. Light reveals the many facets of water and some of what is hidden beneath: seashells, fish or algae. Similarly, the skies are illuminated with rays that reveal layers of cloud and blues shifting between azure and blue-grey or black. All of these find order and logic in David Ohannessian's ceramic tiles. The memories I will carry with me to the afterlife will likely include those same tiles as well as the improvised meals with feta cheese, wine and olives in the Papadimos family garden. It amuses me to think that after all these years, the relevant women in my life are the Platonic women of my Christian names – Jane Austen and the saintly Barbara –but I must refrain from bitter irony at this advanced stage of my life.

I wonder how many of you actually know the origin of the name Barbara. It happens to be my middle name, and its story connects me strongly to the Middle East. Under the Roman rule of Maximilian, in the third century, lived a wealthy merchant named Diascorus in Baalbek, Lebanon. Diascorus went to great lengths both to protect his daughter's virginity and prevent her conversion to Christianity: he built a tower. Whenever he had to travel for several days, he would lock her in the tower. The tower had only two windows, high up. But his daughter helped a local Christian priest open a third, much lower window through which he entered the tower and baptised the girl.

When Diascorus returned from one of his journeys and discovered the third window, he set the tower on fire. His daughter managed to escape and hid in the hills of Baalbek. However, a shepherd betrayed her location in exchange for a large sum of money. Under duress, Diascorus tried to force her to renounce Christianity. But, even though her two breasts were cut off and a burning torch was tied to her body, she kept her faith. To punish her, her father decided to behead her. At that moment, black clouds gathered overhead and a lightning bolt struck and killed him. The girl – the Barbarian, as the Christians called her – became Saint Barbara, after whom I am named.

Is it pretentious to compare Barbara's story to mine? Is it exaggerated and presumptuous to say that I came to the remote

Jerusalem to open a window in a dark tower? In any case, when I took up the post of architect in Jerusalem, some 800 years after the Knights Templar, I knew that it was an opportunity to leave my mark on the holy city. I might have been too young for the role, but the war years left me with scars so deep that I felt old. I was determined to start my life's true mission after leaving behind my wounded comrades and the innumerable bodies over which I had to step. Clearly a new chapter was beginning for me. In fact, not just a new chapter but an entire story.

Note

Austen, Saint-Barb, Harrison – born 1891 in Kent, England, planned and built the Palestine Museum of Archaeology (currently the Rockefeller Museum). He remained in Jerusalem for fifteen years and died in Athens in 1976.

Walter Rubin: Father of Racial Theory in Eretz Yisrael

My father was part of the Zionist leadership in Berlin, during the early days of the twentieth century. I hardly saw him when I was a child. In fact, I was very young when he abandoned my mother and me. Due to the fact my mother was not Jewish, for him I was "the fruit of a regrettable relationship." In those days, notions of racial purity were in vogue. Officially, I still carried his name, and every six months, as a duty-bound German, he regularly paid an allowance to my mother. For all other practical matters, though, my father did not recognize me as his daughter. Not then, at least.

Jews of Palestine, to my father, were the Hebrew race. The hitch was he never managed to learn Hebrew, despite having some of the most outstanding linguists and authors as teachers, and the fact he stayed over forty years—forty years!—in Eretz Yisrael. One might say that languages were not his forte or that the German language had outmaneuvered Walter.

Up to the age of seventeen I lived with my mother, Gisela, right in the middle of Berlin, an apartment on a small alley named Keiser. As I said, I saw very little of Father and, after the age of five, only once. He was a successful attorney, and his name was often in the papers or mentioned by neighbors or brought up by my mother. One might say, brought up despite her wishing not to do so or doing so unawares.

She was clearly still in love with Walter and occasionally told others that he was still in love with her. Altruistic motives, to some extent, could be attributed to Father's abdication. Anti-Semitism was on the rise in Germany, and Father was worried that Mother would become the target of discrimination or even violence, because of her common-law intimacy with a Jew. The fact he was a well-known lawyer only intensified resentment to him by non-Jewish Germans. To many of that period, Walter Rubin was a typical example of Jewish dominance and greed. He was eloquent and persuasive in his law practice, and several of his opponents apparently fell short of that kind of proficiency. This might have frightened certain people or brought about feelings of envy. Mother used to say that his German was razor-sharp, but I myself was not sure that this could be said about a language. She also surprised me by claiming she did not mind in the least being the object of hate or prejudice.Mother was ready to endure everything for the sake of her relationship with my dad, but Father decided to emigrate from Germany, and emigrate alone.

This was often viewed as an admission of defeat, that Father accepted his own inferiority, or that the German establishment had now settled its accounts with him. But Walter had his own ideas about the matter. The Zionist movement was neither widely known in those days nor very popular. It had few Jewish adherents and received little support from non-Jews. The active support it did receive back then came, strangely enough, from Nazi quarters. For them the departure of the Jewish population made a lot of sense and was in line with their own theories. If I am not mistaken, this was the reaction to Zionism in many other countries as well.

I was very young at the time and understood little of all that was happening around me. From time to time, I would find Mother in some obscure corner of the house, all huddled and unable to utter a word. At other times she would repeat incessantly phrases such as, "Walter thinks he knows everything," or "Walter is so shortsighted." She was alluding to my father's superiority toward her, pretending always to know what was best for us all. Concerning the racial theory, Mother felt that, being so set in his ideas, Father had mistaken it for an absolute truth.

Father came for a visit to Berlin just as I turned eleven. He came to see us only in order to show Mum that he was not *heartless*, as she often complained to him in her letters. But the real purpose of the journey, according to her, was altogether different. Walter wished to receive the blessing and acknowledgment of the top German racial theorist, someone nearly venerated in those years: Hans Günther.

Early in the morning Father planned to catch the first train to Jena. Mother insisted that we accompany him up to his very departure from the platform. For me, the noise and putrid vapors and, even more so, the nonstop movement of the crowds was unbearable. Father himself was quite animated, even enthusiastic, as if some inauguration ceremony or initiation rite was at stake. Had I been a proper Jewess at the time, I might have thought of the event as Father's bar mitzvah coming-of-age event. I recall only that he reiterated to Mother that *it was a historical moment* in which the World League was finally welcoming Judaism and that *soon the discrimination of Jews would cease.* "Don't you scientists see that it isn't animals that are at stake here but human beings?" Mother replied. "All this excitement around darn racialism..." Father just smiled and left us standing in the smoky station. Mum was all pale and thought we shouldn't count on seeing him again, ever. I, on the other hand, had quite different fantasies of my own.

Six years later, at the age of seventeen, I was hired as a trainee by the Charlottenburg municipal stables. Occasionally, a number of officers from the German cavalry came to the place. Just before their return to active service, I found out from one of them, Lieutenant Peter, that they were off to Palestine, on a mission to back the Ottoman forces. The First World War was already in its third year, and Turkish authorities were afraid that foreign residents in Palestine were siding with the British enemy. Foreigners, and in particular Jewish ones, were therefore expelled, imprisoned or simply done away with. When I mentioned that my own father lived in Jaffa, Lieutenant Peter assured me the Germans were doing all they could to protect the Jewish minority from Ottoman excesses. Many European residents, he said, were now leaving Palestine by any possible means.

Father's glorious dreams would all be shattered now, I was thinking: the return of the Jews to the Holy Land, the end of prejudice against them, an autonomous existence...Little did I imagine that within a few months, I would be meeting up with Father in Istanbul and, a year later, would be joining him in Eretz Israel.

It is with tremendous pain that I recall Mother's reaction to all those plans. "You are more stubborn and intractable than your father," she told me, and a minute later corrected herself saying my father and I were like two peas in a pod. Just before leaving home, carrying with me only a few articles of clothing in a handbag, a toiletry pouch and my travel documents, Mother nearly lost control of herself, forcibly breaking a glass into countless minute pieces. It was one of the few remaining crystal ones, which now lay unrecognizable on the marble surface of our kitchen counter. As we had a very close relationship, it was difficult for me to see Mother confusing the circumstances of Father's departure with those of my own. As if my trip, too, was a kind of a desertion. Weeks before making the actual decision to leave, I tried to reason with her, pointing out the danger Father was in, mentioning the recent massacre of the Armenians by the Ottomans, who were accusing them of treason and that Father needed a young, strong person by him in times like these. It was to no avail. "Walter abandoned us," she kept telling me."In his eyes you are hardly his daughter. Why you should be regarding him as your father is beyond me when in fact you are total strangers to each other."

She had a certain point there. At no period had I spent more than a few hours in Dad's presence, even when he was still living with us. How could I persuade her, then, that deep inside, somewhere in my own identity, I felt like him, Jewish? I did not dare say anything to her about it.

Mother must have hurt one of her fingers clearing the glass shards on the counter. Her bloodstained handkerchief is the image that has remained with me from that day and that conversation.

It was in an Istanbul hotel that I met up with Father, one in which some German army officials were staying as well, and where German was spoken more than any other language. A number of German families were already with me on the train to Istanbul, intending to join their relatives. Some were traveling together farther east, to Palestine. By the time we reached the hotel, Father had been informed of my impending arrival. Enthusiastically, he introduced me to those present around him. He seemed almost proud to be the father of a grown-up daughter and only rarely corrected some of the expressions I was using, whenever he found them too common or when a turn of phrase was not grammatically quite as it should be. In fact, on the whole he treated me as a young disciple. As a number of people around him regarded Father as a sort of mentor, I did not particularly mind his attitude. I was just happy to have found him.

Besides the hotel, I must admit Istanbul was quite repulsive to me. I could not stand either the crowds on the streets or the filth. Only the hotel meals were to my liking, and of course, the plan that slowly emerged to join Father, as soon as the political situation improved, in the land of Israel. It turned out he had formed good contacts with certain British figures of importance and seemed confident that with some luck, within months, he would be able to return to Jaffa. He enumerated the potential Hebrew teachers he could recommend for me in Berlin, as well as Zionist guides who, eventually, could be my instructors. Only once, quite late at night, when most guests had left for their rooms and we were left on our own, did he mention that the formal side of my conversion would have to be straightened out. Until that very evening, the issue had not crossed my mind. But to Father it was an essential move, even though the subject was a delicate one. I gave no reply but felt as if a malignant tumor had been discovered in me—small perhaps, but one that had to be removed. Nothing more about it was said that evening.

Without studying it in depth, and almost despite myself, I still managed to gather that the races had their particular features, strengths and weaknesses, and that people of the same race got along and operated more efficiently together. The Jews' intention to integrate, or even assimilate, into the German people was a delusion. It would bring about the depletion of the genetic qualities of both races, which might only result in disaster. If I understood right, studies made by Father indicated that even within various Jewish groups that ended up immigrating to Palestine—Diaspora Jews from India, Yemen or Morocco—he detected a weakening of the original stock. One of Zionism's first tasks, according to him, was to attempt a perfection of the Jewish genetic heritage through adequate family planning and intermarriage of Oriental Jews with European ones. He had never stated it openly, but I could conclude from his studies that marriage to an Oriental Jew would be of mutual benefit, even to someone like me, who was only a partial carrier of Jewish genes.

For those Jews who had repeatedly intermarried with non-Jews or those with a physical or a mental disability, Father recommended refusing immigration visas. Quotas for Jews were strictly limited, both before and after the British mandate was in effect, and it would be in line with eugenic principles, according to Walter, to submit careful listings. Father advised me to wait until the political status of Palestine was clarified, and hopefully appropriate contacts would enable me to obtain the necessary documents.

Half of all this rubbish I couldn't take seriously, of course. But the slight chance that I would be embraced by Dad as a full-fledged Jewess, even if only half of the required genes were there, brought me happiness. I returned to Berlin for Hebrew lessons.

All that happened in my life, from the moment I left Germany for good to the end of my father's life, is not really worth narrating. Those were events of a mundane kind, that preoccupy any maturing person. In my relationship with my parents, there were no further drastic changes. My father had become central to the Jewish settlement movement of Palestine, and to an important extent, his ideology had shaped that of the developing bodies of the period: from systematic land purchasing to the treatment of native inhabitants, as well as the attitude toward those Jews arriving from other Arab countries. Only crucial to my story is the last encounter I had with Father, several days just before he died, an encounter that has highlighted for me all the mixed emotions I grew up with since...since I was a little girl, in fact. The sense of emotional conflict increased in me after my father's death to such a degree that it nearly brought about a state of paralysis.

These were the days of the British occupation, and around the globe sentiments of extreme nationalism and prejudice prevailed. The Jewish State was not in existence yet, but all the components, administrative, social and economical, were already laid down. Father claimed he lacked the inner force or physical capacity to continue the struggle. In this respect, the pre-emigration rumors spread in Berlin concerning Walter Rubin's weakness proved to an extent to have some substance to them. I found Father lying in bed, deprived of all force and vitality. His exposed face and hands were almost as white as the bedding covering him.

It should be mentioned, perhaps, that my father had remarried in Palestine and that he had by then not only children from that marriage but grandchildren as well. [In hospital] I had to carefully choose my visiting hours in order to find him alone. A medical assistant stayed by his side almost continuously, but with the nurses I had no difficulty in getting to him.

When I stood by Father's door, I could see he was not asleep, but he made no indication that he noticed me.Only as I approached did I rediscover the piercing eyes I knew so well and the kindness they shone. I so much wished to be held in his arms, as if time had not lapsed since my childhood—or had I ever been held by him this way back then? I couldn't recall. I would have at least bent down to hug him had the pharmaceutical odor in the room not been so intense and the sheets been less perfectly starched. When he finally recognized me, Father whispered, "Just as loyal as your mum, so much more loyal than I've ever been..."

Before I left, Dad gestured with is head to a chest of drawers standing against the wall.

"It is for you, "he said, "a small souvenir..."

I opened the top drawer and discovered a tiny cardboard case.

I did not dare open the small box as I noticed my father's eyes had shut. Till his funeral day, two weeks later, I did not get to see him. Only a cruel and merciless God, or a severely disturbed human being, could have orchestrated events in this way and produced the item that lay in the tiny box. No surreal exhibition—one displaying strange sculpture in certain European galleries, at the time—could have included the one I found. It ought to be noted that the Second World War was at its peak and news of the massive death camps and the manhunt of Jewish families were daily confirmed by British and other sources. The box contained a silver-coated medal. On one side, it had a shining Star of David, and on the other, it had an equally shiny swastika. If any doubts lingered in my mind as to its authenticity, the year 1934, the minting location and details of its silver percentage were all recorded.

After my father's passing away, a devastating depression overtook me.

A Homeland for Two Weeks

"Awaiting you all summer,
Awaiting you all winter"
from "*Habbaitak*," a song by Fairuz

A Palestinian State was declared September 30, 1948, in the city of Gaza. Supported by the Arab League, the Jerusalem mufti Hajj Amin al-Husseini announced its creation, with himself as president. It was recognized by most Arab states. Two weeks later, the mufti moved to an apartment in the outskirts of Cairo, and the government was dissolved.

An acrid disappointment spread among the refugees of the Gaza Strip, one of many that were to come. This held true for the numerous families of the Burge camp I administrated. We Friends, belonging to the Quaker society, were still hoping that in an act of appeasement, the newly created State of Israel would give back some of the territory it had conquered in the previous few weeks. Or, alternatively, that it would allow the population to return to their lands and homes. Instead, Israel brought bulldozers that erased hundreds of villages from the face of the earth.

For the families I was working with, this was the Nakba—massacres, exile, occupation and destruction—all in one word.

We were perched on a *kurkar* sandstone hill, all hard and barren. Nothing green was to be seen in the entire landscape. There was just sand and rock. Even the blue sky weighed heavily upon us: not a cloud in view. I have seen dry places in my life, but nothing compared to those lost hills. The sun baked the surface of the rock, from dawn to dusk, with only a pitiful number of tents offering shade.

The main worry was water: there wasn't any. A Red Cross vehicle transporting a water tank distributed a jerry can a day per family of four. This was meant to allow every one of us two glasses of water and some supply for rudimentary cooking and hygiene. It was difficult to imagine such circumstances could last for more than a few weeks, but as with similar or even worse situations, we found out they could.

I was one of a very few American women in the entire Gaza Strip—some 360 square kilometers—and the only American woman of African descent. Even the poorest and most melancholic displaced person stared at me with a slight smile when encountering a heavy dark woman, wearing a white cotton dress, in the middle of the camp, and particularly when I began speaking in my raspy, quiet English. I didn't care. The half smile they granted me made up for some of their suffering. And in any event, there was just too much work for me to accomplish.

Even now, when I am about to recount all that took place, a kind of embarrassment overcomes me, although at the time, the events were just my manner of coping. Yasser was a young Egyptian doctor, employed by the Red Cross. He spoke reasonable English, and we tended to jest or tease each other whenever possible. There were not many English speakers around, and even fewer folks in a state to joke.

I had my obvious reservations regarding Yasser's behavior. He was an only child, issue to a fairly wealthy family, and as with many male offspring in his situation, he tended to be a bit spoiled and selfish. Worse was the fact he did not really take to the Palestinians. I was surprised that between the Egyptian residents of the strip and the recent Palestinian newcomers—those arriving from such places as Lydda, Bir Sheba and Jaffa or closer-by villages of the Nakab—there was often an noteworthy distancing or even animosity. It was understandable that, being an elite group of some eighty thousand in Palestine's largest and most affluent city, the Egyptians would resent the arrival of some two hundred thousand displaced people. What's more, the inhabitants of Gaza were accustomed to free mobility and open borders, whereas now they were locked in by the Israeli army on the east and the Egyptian army on the south. Almost all connection with the outside world ceased. But witnessing the miserable families that often made their way to Gaza on foot, adults carrying their children or supporting an elderly parent with one hand and holding onto large bags in the other, how could one refuse them water or nourishment, shade or shelter? It raised fury in me, but filled me also with compassion.

In order to channel these feelings and get some answers to my questioning, I invested myself totally in charity work: sorting and distributing food and clothing, creating a dispensary clinic, and compiling and updating lists of the many stateless individuals. Their needs, including health issues and the search for missing family members, were multiple and urgent. Despite my state of exhaustion, frustration and intense activity, I found myself falling in love with Yasser. As often is the case under war and strife, norms change, and it is impossible to pass judgment on a person's conduct. I am not referring to certain inexcusable acts like cruelty, violence or torture. I had to accept my own needs and limitations and learn not to be too hard on myself. I had to be supported and cared for, in order to support and care for others: all those refugees who were in dire straits.

To an extent I got seduced by Yasser. There was such shortage of food and water in the camp that it would have been inhumane to refuse certain occasional gifts from Yasser. For him those gifts represented close to nothing, and I was quite sure it was his family that urged him to offer me a glass of sahleb cream or fresh guava juice once or twice a week. But these little surprises and Yasser's joviality did the job. After a few weeks of us collaborating in the camp, I could not get my mind off him. It was not as if I was no longer concentrating on my tasks or that everyone in the camp became aware of our relationship—far from it. I devoted myself to helping others as never before and did so with real thoroughness. But come evening time, I overcame my exhaustion, wet a towel with a few drops of water (washing oneself properly was out of the question), put some perfume on and felt ready for an adventure.

Our relationship was disrupted by Yasser's frequent trips to Egypt and my own excursions to release supplies or handle other administrative issues. I often had to negotiate with the Israeli authorities on the border or join meetings with UN representatives. These ventures outside of the camp were opportunities to catch up on some sleep and, of course, to take a real shower. There was something desperate in the bind between Yasser and me. He knew that Gaza would never regain its former status and that he should either leave or himself become a Palestinian. I identified so intensely with the Palestinian people and took their catastrophe so much to heart that I could survive and function only under some drug. My drug, at that time, was Yasser.

To the Quakers, as with a number of other bodies or personalities, it was becoming clear that there was no immediate solution for the half-million stateless persons, expelled from their homes, fields and homeland. It was a phenomenon on a huge scale, almost unprecedented in that part of the world. After the help we extended to so many displaced persons in Europe, both Jews and non-Jews, it was hard for us to grasp that those very refugees were now putting on a new outfit, showering and turning into occupiers, similar to the ones they had been victims of a few months earlier.

Yasser and I would leave stealthily in the Red Cross vehicle, me hidden in the back, or him driving with the headlights off. On our way back, I would get out some three hundred meters away from the camp and cover the remaining distance on foot. On other occasions, we left the tents after dark, walking to a lone *kurkar* rock or some ruins we found. Both of us knew the relationship was limited to the particular situation we were in. Fatigue prevented us from any further introspection.

This trancelike existence lasted for nearly a year. Toward the end of this period, the Quaker administrators transferred all camp responsibilities to a newly formed organ called UNWRA. I myself was asked to relocate to the Zeitoon neighborhood of Gaza in order to assist with the creation of a Christian school there. Yasser was given administrative duties in supervising activities of the Red Cross.

In 1950 I met Norman, an American language instructor. Perhaps a divine hand guided me toward a more even view of the conflict, or an ironic twist of fate had its way, but Norman was Jewish. We made up our minds to go back to the United States and get married, in the Friends' tradition. By the time our departure was organized, I was already in my third month of pregnancy. As already mentioned, I was a fairly large woman and therefore did not suspect any signs of my state were visible. Nevertheless, a few days before we left, I received a note from Yasser that left me in some doubt. He begged me not to forget Palestine, said he was ashamed of his previous attitude to all the stateless families we worked with and suggested I name my first child Seif, in case it was a boy, or Nur, if a girl. *Seif* was the sword the refugees required for their struggle, and *Nur* was the light at the end of the tunnel.

Six months later I held in my arms the most beautiful baby I have ever seen. We called her Nur.

Sheikh Munis

Part One

Simon was the youngest of the De-el Brothers. This was the *nom de guerre* given them by the French Resistance, partially in order to gloss over their obvious Jewish name. *De-el* sounded a bit like *de Gaulle* but was in fact the initials of Simon's older brother, David Levi.

Regardless of Simon's young age—he was only seventeen when he joined the Resistance in North Africa, toward the middle of World War Two—he became, soon enough, an explosives expert. Now that the war was over, the Hagannah, in Palestine, was happy to recruit youngsters such as David and Simon, those with some combat experience. But Simon preferred to remain in Europe.

He was a rather short, pale and skinny boy, and the elderly ladies at the Belvedere would point him out whenever Simon showed up in the Jewish Parents' home in Brussels, which doubled also as coordination point for the Hagannah:

« *Il est de retour, le beau garçon...* »

A guy nicknamed *the Bleached* was expecting Simon at the small side-wing of the building.

"I am trained as a gun-care specialist," Simon told him, "not a child-care one. What the Hagannah really requires at the Hapo-el camp is a social worker."

"Come on, Simon, don't exaggerate. The volunteers are the same age as you, if not older."

"According to the Red Cross lists, you might be right," Simon agreed, "but in reality they don't have a clue. They lack any motivation for either self-defense or the use and maintenance of arms. I would never entrust a weapon to any of them."

"This educational task can't be easy for you after Algiers," said the Bleached, "but there is a mission I could possibly interest you in. You said Palestine was not for you, at this point, as your mother lives on her own in Lyons. What would you say to a Marseille–Haifa job? You could call on your brother David in Binyamina, and a few days later check on your mother, once you are back in France."

"Wow,"said Simon, "the Hagannah is becoming a real travel agency..."

"Something like that, "said the Bleached. "We will need a number of boys to accompany boats full of immigrants. Two of our boats are undergoing renovation in Naples and two in Marseilles.

"This is the best offer I've had since de Gaulle's *France Libre*."

To finalize all the details of the new employment, Simon and the Bleached sat down for lunch at the Hagannah's table, in the old people's dining hall. Some of the elderly nodded their heads whispering. The Bleached told Simon, "No need for much social-work training to improve people's humor..."

Simon spent the following weekend in Lyons, strolling the streets leading down to the Rhoan River, the neighborhood where he grew up. He discovered anew things that had disappeared during the war, such as khale bread or apple cake at the Jewish baker's. When his mother suggested he join her at the Ashkenazi synagogue on Tilsit Quay, Simon told her that Yiddish reminded him too much of German. Of course less than a minute later he regretted what he had said. Yiddish was the language his parents spoke at home, before his father was sent to Auschwitz.

On Monday, he crossed over the newly opened Gallieni Bridge, leading to the Perrache station. Smoke, mingled with morning mist, obscured the platforms. During the long trip, Simon busied himself repairing a small Monarch Morse-code transmitter the Bleached had handed to him in Brussels. Only on the last stretch of the ride did he manage to take a nap on the uncomfortable hard seats. As agreed the previous week, once he got to Marseilles Simon took a taxi in order to avoid being followed. He told the driver to drop him a few streets away from the port, where the Hagannah had its headquarters.

Part Two

The boat called *Asia* left Marseilles Wednesday morning. All through the previous night the illegal immigrants were assembled in two boat-repair hangars. They were instructed to take along provisions for twenty-four hours and, advisedly, use the toilet before arriving at the port. Only when the rain had ceased and total darkness engulfed the various abandoned buildings, some two hundred men and women, with perhaps a handful of children, crossed over from the quay onto the boat, using movable metal stairs. The older passengers, and those few couples with children, were given cabins. All the rest were split into groups of ten, nominated their contact person, and were assigned a corner of the boat where they could settle with their affairs. Zvi was a volunteer physician from Germany who, together with another doctor and two nurses, formed the medical team for the journey.

The Greek staff of thirteen sailors and cooks was more than a little surprised to find out the boat was not headed to Lisbon for maintenance, as they had been told, but to an undisclosed port in the east of the Mediterranean. Naturally, the presence of so many unofficial passengers was even more startling for them. During the first hot meal, the atmosphere quickly flared up in the kitchen of the boat. When Simon was sent to calm things down, inadvertently or not a pot of boiling soup slid onto a trolley, spilling a third of its contents on Simon's arm. Pleas coming from all sides for Simon to rush to the dispensary were awkwardly ignored by him. Instead, he just sat down to have supper with the others, as if nothing had occurred.

Straight after the meal, Zvi was instructed to examine Simon in the Hagannah's office, but his limited French was not all that helpful.

"I am Zvi," he said, "from the Mahal, "which were overseas volunteers.

"Well, " Simon replied.

« *Moi medecin, voir ta main...* »

The doctor's pronunciation and grammar were so off that Simon had to smile.

"I noticed you were with the Berlin volunteers," he told Zvi."I myself speak some Yiddish."

"Yiddish and German are not the same," Zvi said in German, "but it is worth a try."

"I did not imagine a youngster like you could be a doctor already. It is not just a case of false diplomas or something, is it?"

"Let's examine your arm, instead of you playing superman," Zvi replied. "It smells like roasted meat in here..."

Indeed, Simon's arm was not in great shape, but it was an opportunity for Simon and Zvi to get to know each other. Without the injury, Simon would have avoided the German speakers, and Zvi, although a physician, was not included in the close-knit circle of the combating Hagannah members.

"The other doctor looks like Frankenstein to me," Simon said, "and the nurses seem like they are in need of a doll to play with. I will manage the arm well on my own, once you finish with the bandages."

"I will come in person every morning," Zvi replied. "At what time do the Hagannah warriors wake up?"

"From four to five in the morning, you may find me here in the office."

"After I am through with your arm, it will be the insomnia that I will have to deal with," Zvi suggested, tongue-in-cheek.

"This word does not exist in Yiddish," Simon said laughing.

Part Three

When the English mandate forces dragged the *Asia* to the so-called shadow port in Haifa, sending the illegal immigrants to a detention camp in Atlit, the Hagannah managed to smuggle out its own staff members. Simon had persuaded those responsible to include Zvi in the group disguised as port workers. This saved Zvi a few weeks of misery in Atlit.

The very next day, Zvi and Simon made it to Binyamina, to visit Simon's brother.

"I am meant to join the Mahal office on Meltset Street," Zvi said in answer to David's question.

"Where would that be?"

"In Tel Aviv, I believe."

"And from there, where?"

"It was planned I would be practicing as a doctor in a town called Sheikh Munis."

"Which is where?"

"Near Tel Aviv...if I am not mistaken."

"In case you mean the Sheikh Munis I know," David told Zvi, "by now the town exists only on paper. A bit like the *shtetels* of Eastern Europe."

"A few weeks back, I was given to understand there was a thriving community there. That is what Mahal representatives told me in Germany."

"At the moment there are just empty houses," David said.

"And the inhabitants?" Zvi inquired.

"As Ben-Gurion indicated in his universal sign-language—" and here Simon's brother gestured with his hand in the air, imitating clouds carried by the wind "—they are all gone.

"Were there many of them in Sheikh Munis?"

"A few thousand," David replied.

Sheikh Munis was the largest Palestinian settlement, just north of Tel Aviv. It covered both sides of the Uja River, known also as the Yarkon. Its orchards supplied a large part of all citrus exports from Jaffa. Because of Sheikh Munis's proximity to Tel Aviv, the Hagannah decided to barricade its central area, erecting a checkpoint at the entrance to control the population. Fearing this was one step short of liquidation, all Sheikh Munis's inhabitants fled as soon as skirmishes and bombing intensified around the village.

Part Four

All sorts of leftovers from the Great War in Europe made their way to the Hagannah's office in Tel Aviv—Russian, German, English and American weapons—an office that became for a time Simon's personal amusement park. He accompanied five different cruise boats during those days and, from time to time, instructed volunteers in sabotage and the handling of arms. Occasionally he visited his new friend Zvi in what was once the village of Sheikh Munis. It had recently been transformed into a Jewish military base.

"Never did I imagine myself as a physician in a ghost town," Zvi told Simon during one of those encounters.

"And now?" Simon prompted.

"Now I am almost a combat hotshot like you," Zvi joked."Soldiers seem to like me, and it is only the Hebrew language that gets in the way..."

"I, on the other hand, am looking for a full-time position in France," Simon said. "Fooling around was pleasant, but enough is enough. This place is preparing itself for an ongoing war. It is the right time for me to leave."

"Honestly," said Zvi, "I am not quite fit for this country either. It changes a person in strange ways. I went to see two cousins of mine, settled in the North, and I could hardly recognize them. They have become like strangers."

"My brother, too, is no longer French," Simon said.

During long months in 1948, Simon made attempts to return to France, distancing himself from the Hagannah, which had now become the Israeli Defense Army. Events, though, were rolling faster than he was: war was everywhere. As nothing was heard from his brother who was in combat in the Negev, Simon agreed to join a so-called French Commando team of temporary volunteers, searching for missing soldiers. As soon as battles abated, David, Simon's brother, made his way back to Binyamina. It turned out he had been held prisoner for a short while by a Bedouin tribe. On his way home, he mailed a postcard, displaying one of the first stamps printed by the Israeli state.

To the military medical authorities, Attention Doctor Zvi Grunberg,
Sheikh Munis Camp, the Tel Aviv vicinity.
Dear Zvi, my brother Simon was critically wounded
and died in the Be'er Sheva hospital on August 31. David Levi.

Part Five

As a souvenir from Simon, Zvi had only a hand-operated Dynamo pocket flashlight. In 1949 he received an invitation to join a hospital in New Jersey. There was a significant Jewish community in the hospital area. On his way to the port of Rotterdam, he made a point of stopping in Lyons. He no longer had any family of his own in Europe. Before leaving Israel for good, he took from David the address of Roza Levi, the mother of David and Simon.

When he knocked on her door, his head went blank. The few sentences in Yiddish he had rehearsed in advance had all disappeared. Roza was pale and small, just like Simon, but remnants of very dark hair, similar to David's, showed here and there through the white strands. It was especially her black eyebrows that struck Zvi. Roza embraced Zvi as if she had known him long before and pulled his head onto her shoulder. Indeed, Zvi felt as if his head had become as heavy as the military kitbag bearing his name in white paint, the kitbag he had been carrying for the past two years of volunteering from the port in Marseilles to Sheikh Munis and from there back to Marseilles. Finally he managed one broken phrase in Yiddish."Simon was my best friend, and he was like a brother to me." It might have sounded to Roza like a stutter, but that was all that was said between them. On his way out of Roza's home in Lyons, Zvi left behind—just by the black Bakelite telephone—Simon's metallic Dynamo light.

Amina

Dear Sir,

My name is Amina, and I am twelve years old. None of my neighbors or acquaintances seem to think there is any point in writing you. They are all sure my letter will remain unread. I write to you anyhow.

It is a month now that we have resided in Al Aqaba. Our own home in Um Al Rashrash is occupied by the Jews. Now we have only a tent and use municipal toilets, together with the other families.

My father has been employed by the British authorities since before I was born. He has documents in English from all the training courses he took in the 1940s. He does not understand how, from one day to the next, Um Al Rashrash turned from a village under British rule to a pile of ruins under the Israelis. He already wrote you but received no answer. My mom cannot stop crying because all our belongings remain at home and we are prevented from returning there. People tell us we are lucky to be alive and our losses are only material ones. Still, my mother does not stop crying.

Before we left, we were told the war was over. With my own ears I heard English soldiers saying there was nothing further to fear, Palestine has fallen into Jewish hands, Jaffa and Jerusalem included, but Um Al Rashrash is out of reach. It is only a small and insignificant spot, they said. We were also told the Nakab desert has so much sand that no jeep, or even a tank, could pass through it. It is true there is much sand there, even in Um Al Rashrash. But to say it is unimportant is wrong. There are only a few houses, and there were no shops or factories, but Um Al Rashrash has the sea. The sea is as large as the desert. The sea has all the life that the desert does not. There are fish and crabs and eels. There are dolphins and sharks. Lots of birds come there, and boats arrive from all sorts of places. How can one say it is insignificant?

We had our own school, with fourteen pupils all in one classroom. There were boys and girls of all ages. We had a good teacher, who even spoke English. Sometimes, we would bake bread with him on embers buried in the sand. This was the activity my brother liked the most. I preferred English. This is how I am able to write you now. I did not attend school for four years for nothing. My father already mentioned to you that the lime whitewash for the walls, the blackboard, the books and writing supplies, as well as the teacher's salary were all for nothing if Um Al Rashrash is handed over to the occupier and the population is chased away.

The war was already over, but still you let soldiers get to Um Al Rashrash. The cease-fire agreement was signed. Men in our village drank coffee to mark the end of hostilities. Women wished to celebrate but knew that too many families paid with their lives and that others were expelled. Then the soldiers showed up in our village, as if the war had just begun. They told us to pack our things and go. It did not help that women and children were begging to stay.

If there weren't the barbed wires and army posts, I could see our home from here, from Jordan. Had they allowed me to, I would have swum from Al Aqaba beach to Um Al Rashrash. I could have seen the fishing boats left behind and the family of brown dogs. The bitch had a litter of four the week we left. The sea is so shallow in places, one can even walk along the beach to reach our home from here.

I am writing you because we were hoping to return. I left food for our chickens and cats, but only enough for one week. Now a whole month has gone by and still we are not allowed back. I am worried the animals have nothing to eat or to drink. When people are dying, perhaps you'd think eight chickens, a cock and three cats are nothing. But I heard that British people care for pets. Together with our teacher we read in the *Jerusalem Post* that in Jerusalem an animal cemetery for your deceased dogs and cats was created. One of our own cats, the gray and white one, was very dear to me. I called her Whitey. She followed us everywhere and wanted to join us when we left.

I beg you to check what happened to the animals we left behind in Um Al Rashrash. If we have to stay in Jordan much longer, the animals might die. The water bucket in the garden needs to be filled for them as well. Is someone surveying the empty houses? Are English authorities allowed to approach the village? I am also worried Israeli soldiers might eat our chickens.

I thank you for your help and hope you will reply soon. Sincerely,

Amina A-Din, UNWRA Al Forege Camp, Al Aqaba, Jordan.

Historical note:

Um Al Rashrash was one of the last locations to be annexed by Israel in 1949. The city of Eilat would be built right next to the village. Al Aqaba is the Jordanian Red Sea port city, facing Eilat.

The Mold

Unlike the houses flanking, instead of a roof terrace, the stone house of the Razal family had a small balcony facing the street. A large carob tree and a very small lemon tree managed to survive in the back garden, and a rope tied between the two served the household for hanging laundry. Their home was situated in the town of Ibn Gariye, roughly a two-hour walk from Marrakech.

Yona reports that her dad acquired the French language in the Alliance School and was later employed by the local colonial administration as a clerk. It was he who insisted on the Western look of the home he built for the family.

In 1950 Yona married Saya (Sa'adia) Zadik, who was a native of a small village in the Atlas Mountains, and they settled in Yona's parents' home, where their own three children were born. The roots of the Razal family were partially in the same mountainous area as Saya's and partially from villages closer to Agadir, on the coast. The family tree went back hundreds of years, and it was likely the ancestors reached Morocco back in Roman times.

Regarding her wedding in Demnat and the visits to holy burial grounds and to various waterfalls, Yona talks with delicacy, as if she was threading pearls of a precious bracelet. She recalls her youth and childhood as peaceful periods, with relationships between Jewish and Muslim families being warm and close. On special occasions, she said, her family would travel to Marrakesh, where a number of synagogues and a large Jewish community were to be found. The market area in Marrakesh, the bazaar, Yona remembers as a magical place, as if it had sprung out of a fairy tale. Entire streets throbbed to the rhythm of blacksmiths, in souk Attarin, or that of carpenters, in the Nejjarin. Other alleys were taken over by cobblers, weavers, jewelers or basket makers. Fortune tellers, musicians, trained monkeys and even a dancing bear made their way to the main square from various parts of Northern Africa.

Yona and Saya had two sons, Reuben and Victor, and one daughter, Ester. All three went to the local kindergarten and schools. As in those years opposition to the French rule increased, some Jews like Yona's father felt threatened because of their affiliation with the French. The establishment of the State of Israel and the active interference of Zionist bodies in internal Moroccan affairs only aggravated matters. Even minor groups, such as the Lubavitch, infiltrated small Jewish communities, criticizing their form of religious practice.

Yona and Saya did not face any particular financial difficulties, even though earnings from Saya's fish deliveries were not abundant or steady. He was happy, nevertheless, to make his rounds, waking up before sunrise, driving down to the coast for a couple of hours and returning with a vanload of fresh fish. The rest of the day was his to spend with his family or in the Wifak offices where he was active.

At the end of January 1956, the year the French left Morocco incidentally, Saya died. Due to heavy frost, the road was slippery and Saya's van slid down one of the steepest slopes. A few months later, Yona's father lost his clerical work, following Morocco's recent independence. These events left the family in dire straits, only managing through the few translation jobs Yona's father managed to obtain and the cooking Yona herself did for various clients. She vehemently opposed sending the children to the Lubavitch boarding school, but for four years she had to endure mounting pressure from the Zionist movement to enroll the children in their activities.

The year 1960 was decisive: it was a time of upheaval for the Zadik family, to such an extent that Yona would find it difficult to fully recover from it for many years to come. Representatives of the Jewish Agency were active throughout the country, despite being officially banned in Morocco. Code words were used by the agents in order to disguise the nature of their objectives. Recruitment was coded *Ballet Dancing*, self-defense training was termed *Kindergarten Knocks*, and illegal immigration was called *Choir Performance*. The entire presence of the agency in Morocco was referred to as *the Mold*.

Victor was nine at the time, and Reuben ten, and Yona had agreed that they could join the Zionist Summer Camp. In her worst dreams, it wouldn't have occurred to her that without their parents' knowledge or any identity or immigration documents, the children might end up on an airplane to Israel, organized by the Mold. It took her months to find out where the boys were, and she realized she might never get to see them again. Bribes paid to various officials and false papers and visas enabled the Mold to smuggle hundreds of Jews out of North Africa, including many unaccompanied children like Reuben and Victor.

Yona's agony was only beginning, and the year was not yet through. President Nasser of Egypt arrived on a state visit to Casablanca. Enthusiastic demonstrations of support soon escalated into anti-Zionist and anti-Jewish protests. Yona's sister, with her husband and children, made the decision to immigrate to France. Like little Reuben and Victor they, too, were kidnapped by the Mold, the boat they boarded rerouted in the middle of the sea. Things went wrong, and the boat reached neither France nor Israel. A coral reef was in the boat's way, and all its passengers ended up drowning.

Stricken by grief and worry, Yona accepted the Mold's offer to immigrate to Israel, in order to locate her sons. She was forced to leave her parents behind, though, as the Jewish Agency refused to subsidize the journey of an elderly couple. For weeks she and little Ester had to stay in a displacement camp, with poor sanitary conditions, leaky huts and no news about her sons. It turned out the boys were now attached to a kibbutz, as external residents. Reuben had been diagnosed with polio, and it was recommended he remain in the kibbutz for further treatment. Victor joined his mother and sister in temporary lodging near Jerusalem. When Yona found out an abandoned Palestinian neighborhood was occupied by recent comers from Marrakesh, she arranged for her family to settle in one of the empty houses. On top of no official reliable, running water and electricity, the big hitch was the location: it turned out the neighborhood was situated on the very border between East and West Jerusalem. When hanging laundry on the roof to dry or when the children went out to play by the no-man's-zone, snipers' bullets occasionally were fired at them.

The Jerusalem architect David Redlich designed and supervised the building of the first supermarket in the city, as well as the modern residential units above it. His son Raphael was Victor's age, but the boys never met. While Raphael was attending school, Victor was collecting empty bottles in order to receive their consignment value at the newly opened supermarket. Yona, on the other hand, knew the Redlichs well: she was the architect's cleaning woman. Once trust grew between Yona and Rachel Redlich, from time to time after work she was allowed to use their shower. Yona was even welcome to bring her children occasionally, as in their Musrara home there was neither hot water nor showers. Victor rarely made it to school, and even his Hebrew was rudimentary at that point. When he turned fourteen, Mr. Redlich arranged for him to be employed by the building contractor he was working with. From then on he was able to take his showers in the portable sanitary blocks at the building sites.

In Raphael's high school in Rehavia nothing was said of the Wadi Salib riots in Haifa, riots organized by North African Jews to protest against discrimination in housing and employment. Perhaps Raphael's parents did not even know about the riots. When Raphael completed his final exams and was drafted for his military service, Victor was busy protesting in front of the Jerusalem municipal building. There was talk of the *second Wadi Salib* events. Except in Jerusalem, instead of hundreds of demonstrators there were thousands present. Of Victor and his friends, the prime minister said that they were "not very nice children." Yona, however, felt he was an adorable child.

For ten years the Zadik family stayed in the abandoned Palestinian house. Having been an activist in the protest movement, Victor became a political leader. Taking after the North American group, they called themselves the Panthers. Victor still did not fit into the mold.

Coexistence in Sfar'am

Unlike many of the stories included in this compilation, the present one is not politically engaged and, as a result, is perhaps the only normal story of the lot. The Russian author Tolstoy remarked that stories concerning normal families are utterly boring (I am undoubtedly misquoting him here), but in our utterly abnormal country, it is likely that a normal story will be considered quite exceptional. It was told to me by a Druze couple, settled in the Netherlands in the 1970s. Druze, by the way, if I understand correctly, prefer being called *Elmuwahidun*, meaning *the Monotheists*. From their story, I inferred they chose to tell me this particular one as a gesture of acceptance toward me. Or rather, as an indication they didn't resent me for being Jewish. Although the couple now led a secular life, they came from the traditional city of Shfar'am, which had witnessed mutual living of Muslims, Christians, Jews and Druze for generations, free of hatred, clashes or feuds. Inhabitants used Arabic in their day-to-day dealings, and Hebrew was spoken only in the synagogue, the building of which still stands to this very day in the center of town. The last Jewish residents left Shfar'am in the 1940s.

One of Shefa Amr's most illustrious leaders, or *mukhtar*, had a son named Ali. *Shefa Amr*, incidentally, is the Arabic form of *Shfar'am*. Ali was a good-looking, well-educated young man, but he had a tendency to daydream. He loved nature and, as the heir in a well-to-do family, he was able to spend entire days wandering the trails of the region: climbing cliffs and hills, descending mountainsides and frequenting caves and waterfalls. When the *mukhtar* and his wife decided it was time their son Ali got married, a match was arranged with another local Muslim family—not an exceedingly rich one, but definitely not a line of poor peasants. It was felt that acquiring a trade would do Ali good and that he would have to earn a living in order to support his wife and children. The long procedure preceding the marriage began in earnest: determining an adequate dowry; fixing a fine in case, God forbid, the couple did not get along and separated; and planning the three days of wedding celebrations. Ali seemed to go along with his parents' decision, accepting the engagement, yet refraining from any active contribution to all the preparations. After the religious ceremony had taken place, and the Qadi recited the *khutbah* of marriage—and only a few weeks before the wedding feasts were to take place—all came to a halt. To everyone's stupefaction and disappointment, Ali entered a state of deep slumber, a kind of a trance or even a coma. All efforts to return him to reality failed.

Ali's father, the Shefa Amr *mukhta*r, consulted the local sheikh and the Muslim healers, and when they couldn't wake Ali up, he went to the Aakel Druze wise men, the Christian priests and the Jewish rabbi. Each and every one of them prayed for Ali's health, organized meditations, and sprinkled holy water or furnished amulets. Nothing was of any help.

Ali's bride, Suraya, who feared remaining a deserted wife should Ali's state not alter, took matters into her own hands. She was, perhaps, the most practical and resourceful of those surrounding Ali. On the whole, ties among Shefa Amr's women, regardless of the community they belonged to, were extremely close. Events such as weddings, circumcisions or the numerous holidays were moments of communion and exchange between families. The fact that Ali had visited Bedouin settlements in the area was cause for many rumors and speculations concerning possible spells having been put on him or even infections he might have been exposed to. Many of the women suggested remedies, amulets or counter spells Suraya might try. When all these trials came to nothing, and possibly out of frustration at the cancellation of the three days of feasts with their sumptuous meals, the idea of a culinary treatment arose, incorporating the rich foods Shefa Amr was renowned for. If a certain food appealed to Ali, they argued, perhaps it would draw him out of his state. Each community had its special dishes, and in their meetings the women reviewed this vast heritage. A simple cabbage would offer itself to some forty recipes, including the much appreciated stuffed *Malfoof*, and desserts numbered in the hundreds, many of them, such as the *Qatayef* and the *Matabbaq*, involving honey and pistachios, which were meant to have a healing effect. With the help of so many sympathizing neighbors, Suraya prepared many of these appealing offerings and laid them in front of Ali. But despite all this, the situation remained desperate.

Absent from those women's gatherings was the rabbi's wife, Hodaya. She was a somewhat private person, who admitted to her home only those few women who were in great need or distress. Hodaya was no great cook and therefore found little interest in sharing recipes or kitchen experiences with her neighbors. It wasn't that she was haughty or self-important, but she was known for the seriousness and concentration required for her consultations to families in need. It was not rare that she would even give advice to her husband when he faced some seemingly insurmountable difficulty. This was how she became aware of Ali and Suraya's situation. She consented to join the quest for a remedy, for by now the matter had evolved into a collective mystery.

It transpired that Ali was slightly asthmatic and often held his mouth open, even while sleeping. Also, whenever he went on a prolonged hike, he was in the habit of taking a snack with him and settling for a small meal and a rest, lying alongside some waterfall or spring. There he would while away an hour or two, until the great heat of the day was over, and head back to Shefa Amr just before sunset. Quite a few rivers or tributaries made their way from the hilltops down to the Mediterranean basin, culminating anywhere between Acre and Haifa or even farther south. Ali was always on his own but would encounter laborers or shepherds on his way. Some of them would notice him taking a nap by a stream or a pool.

While the Arabian viper or adder was known to every child in Shefa Amr because of its size or venomousness, tens of other snakes, much less known, were to be found all over the Galilee. Despite their minute size or unobtrusive features, some snakes could still harm and even kill the person they bit. Hodaya had a profound dread of snakes, and her first reaction to Ali's state was that he had in fact been bitten. The fact that Ali would lie sometimes on the ground with his mouth slightly open suggested to her the possibility that he might have swallowed a small one, while having a rest. Hodaya knew this was a long shot, but taking into consideration his condition, anything was worth a try.

A bucket of boiling water was placed just under Ali's face, water that contained poisonous herbs and bitter oils. After a few moments of having breathed the vapors, Ali began coughing, and it was feared he would suffocate. Convulsions and difficulty in breathing followed, and this extreme treatment was about to be abandoned when suddenly a tiny snake of unknown color slipped out of his mouth, together with phlegm and spittle. Ali immediately opened his eyes, as if just waking up from an afternoon nap by the local Sursok spring.

All those present clapped their hands in amazement and uttered cries of joy and relief. Hodaya returned directly home, making no big deal of the matter. Muttering, as if to herself, she said, "Those abominable snakes! If one takes no precautions, they get everywhere."

Preparations for the wedding were taken with added energy. The celebrations had an intoxicating effect on everyone, even though not a single drop of alcohol was served or consumed. Ali matured considerably and learned the trade of a smith after the feasts ended. Four children were eventually born to Suraya and him: two boys and two girls. The unusual story remained on everyone's mind, not just for weeks or months but years. It continues to be told by Druze, Muslims, Christians and Jews, listeners holding their breath when the sequence about the tiny snake is reached. So you are not the only ones, then...

The Rais

For six weeks the Rais lay in his Mansheyet al Bakri home, the very place he had acquired with his wife while still an officer in the Egyptian army. In the national newspaper *Al Ahram*, it was reported that he had the flu. Only a year later, after he passed away, and once the Arab League summit was concluded, was it admitted that Nasser had already had several heart attacks, the last being fatal.

In the simple abode of Mansheyet al Bakri, when Tahia his wife was twenty-seven years old, they already had three children and Tahia was pregnant with their fourth child. The war in Palestine had just ended, but Gamal Nasser did not return from the battles. His wife feared she would be a widow with four children. Nasser, himself, thought he had reached the end. In a scrapbook he used as a diary during his capture in Faluja (today Kiryat Gat), he noted, *The way to freedom will be long and winding, and it is unlikely I will get even a glimpse of the longed-for day*.

Years later, already approaching his third war, the Rais had his first heart attack. Suffering his second one, his private doctors refused to take any risks and insisted he keep to his bed. For someone used to eighteen-hours days, staying in bed was torture.

"They make me experience Faluja all over again, just like in 1948.Then, too, I was helpless. Israeli soldiers clamped down on us, and we were immobilized for weeks, stuck in the Nakab desert dunes."

To his intimate acquaintances he said that, just as in Faluja, he could see death from up close.

"If there is a nightmare I dread," Nasser told his wife Tahia, "it is leaving you and the children on your own."

As a boy of eight, Nasser's mother died while giving birth to his younger brother. At the time, he was living with his grandparents in Cairo in order to attend school, and the bad news was concealed from him. As letters from her failed to arrive, young Gamal began fearing for his mother's health. Only upon his return from Cairo did he realize the bitter truth. The trauma lasted for weeks on end, the boy unable to utter a single word.

"There are things," he said, after becoming the Rais, "there are things one cannot overcome."

Now that he was lying in bed, he told Tahia, "Without the Egyptian woman, the country would have dissolved in the dunes of the desert long ago. Or: What would I have done without you?"

Two of the first objectives the Rais strove for were the schooling of Egyptian girls and universal medical treatment for the whole population. When Tahia felt he was in the appropriate mood to receive criticism,[6] she would reply, "If the Egyptian woman is so fabulous, how come she chops off her daughter's clitoris?"

The Rais had a profound love for the Egyptian people, but he did not always come up with helpful or practical plans for them.

"Let time take its course," he said. "Sooner or later these women will learn."

Tahia would get him a French journal to read, as the Rais enjoyed practicing his foreign languages by reading the press.

The Rais was of modest origins, his father having been a postal clerk. He, himself, had barely completed his high-school studies, although he lasted a few months of law school. Nasser might have feared he wouldn't witness modern Egypt's glory, but he was the one to disengage Britain's hold on the country in 1956. It was perhaps one of the last instances of the effect of the British Empire there. Nasser was also the one to negotiate the bind between most Arab countries and the initiator of the affinity with such third-world nations as India, Indonesia and Yugoslavia.

Following the Rais's third heart attack, it was difficult for Tahia and her husband to communicate. Nasser returned home from the Arab League conference, but he was constantly surrounded by doctors, his condition not permitting conversation. Only with his eyelids and intense stare did Nasser signal that he recognized his wife. In the sitting room next door, Tahia lowered the record-player needle onto Umm Kulthum's "*Ataf Habibi*." She knew that it was this particular song that was performed for soldiers returning from Faluja. Tahia also knew that her husband wished to be like Umm Kulthum. All of Egypt listened to her, rich and poor. He wished all of Egypt, rich and poor, to listen to him.

At six in the evening, the Rais's eyelashes ceased fluttering, and his lower lip trembled for the last time. During the funeral, along the Nile River, six million men and women followed his coffin.

He was not always logical and was often stubborn, but Nasser knew how to be warm and supportive, like a father. Egypt was his family. Now that he had passed away, a new era had begun for the country, a post-family like era.

Karameh

We'd gotten married just the previous year, and I was already in the fifth month of my pregnancy. The gynecologist in Amman said I was carrying twins and, in fact, was bigger than many other women in my condition. Adnan was ecstatic, and together with friends from Al-Karameh they joked endlessly about his efficiency ("Two for the price of one"), on the deal Adnan and I allegedly agreed on: to have a son and a daughter, rather than a daughter only (as I had wanted). But all this was just joking around. What to me was truly funny was that Adnan and I had met each other when we were just eight or nine years old. His father was a cousin of my mom's, but the two families seldom got together. His family was settled near Ramallah, and we lived in Jerusalem. Nevertheless, I was probably in love with Adnan from that age on. But then, the war came into the midst of it all.

The A-Din Family

The residences of the extended A-Din family sprawled along the two sides of the Old City's southern wall, Silwan Gate acting, as it were, as a link between the relatives. My side of the family was probably the poorest of the A-Dins, and we could not afford leaving the squalid inner walls of Jerusalem. Those that moved up in the world had built themselves houses in Silwan itself. Our own quarter was called the Maghreb, and tradition had it that the A-Dins originated from Tunisia. Around the age of eight, a big family gathering took place in Bani Zeid, on the outskirts of Ramallah. It was a rare occasion for my family to embark on an excursion and see another part of Palestine. It was the first time Adnan and I saw each other, although probably not a single word was exchanged between us. Nevertheless, his delicate features must have made an impression on me.

Different cousins of varying degrees took interest in me from the age of fourteen onward. As our family had limited means (my father being a stonemason), most candidates for engagement to me were poor, just like us. My own objection was not the financial background of those cousins but their education. I had won a scholarship to Beir Zeit College, which I wished to attend, and I had high grades at school. But would there be a candidate willing to marry a person better-educated than himself? Most of them had hardly completed their high-school studies. Despite the fact classes were separated in the Schmidt Institute, which I had just graduated from, I met some nice boys there. No lasting relationships developed with any of them, though. Adnan's eyes followed me, so to speak.

Our own quarter in Jerusalem was extremely crowded but had its particular charm. It had an ancient mosque, small schools and countless merchants and peddlers that offered to sell everything one required. There were also tons of tourists, and many of the neighborhood's women were hired in the guesthouses as cleaners, cooks and receptionists. Come evening, the muezzin called all believers to prayer, and the city was transformed from a busy, noisy, urban agglomerate to a sleepy village. The last of the porters and sweepers would make their way to the central courtyard to wash off the dust and sweat, and calm would descend on the old walls. One by one, minarets lit up their tentative lights, and homes and coffee shops intermittently followed suit. In the distance, isolated church towers rang their bells. The city dissolved into the surrounding hills.

The Bargouti Family

Before fleeing Jaffa, Adnan's family was quite well-to-do. Once the city was occupied in 1947, all of his relatives escaped to their summer residence in Bani Zeid. They thought it was only a temporary move, persuaded that once the battles ceased, all families would return to their Jaffa homes, regardless which side had the upper hand. Destiny had it otherwise. For the majority of those who fled Jaffa, the road back was barred. Like so many other residents, Adnan's family was prevented from returning home. Their property was confiscated, but unlike thousands of others, they were lucky to be in possession of a secondary residence. Adnan's father managed to reestablish himself as an importer of foreign goods in Ramallah, and Adnan's brother was employed there as manager, allowing Adnan to continue his schooling.

In fact, Adnan remembered me only vaguely. Besides me, there were six other female cousins-once-removed, but at the tender age of nine, each time there was a family event, he set more importance on the two soccer teams he organized with his male cousins. Adnan did recall, though, that his Jerusalem relatives' Arabic sounded different from that of the countryside, and that my sister and I giggled constantly when we could not be understood. In 1967 the relations between the different relatives was brought to an abrupt halt.

War

Even before we had time to recover from the shelling, machine guns spraying the streets, the smoke and flames rising from stores and vehicles, the sound of bulldozers, trucks and other demolition equipment invaded the neighborhood. There were perhaps twenty or thirty engines that made a terrible noise. We received orders to abandon all houses and disappear. From all our belongings and valuables we had one hour to form reasonable bundles to carry with us, but in the great confusion we hardly knew what to do or where to go. Those residents who declared themselves unwilling to evacuate their homes got buried under the rubble. This convinced us to rush out of there. The entire Maghreb quarter—hundreds of people of all ages, and about one hundred buildings—all was cleared in two or three days.

I was nearly eighteen then, about to finish my high-school studies that very month. Books and other supplies for my first year of college were already piled in a corner of the house, but from in an instant I was left with nothing. No clothes, no furniture, no money. It was Jordanian army trucks that brought everyone to Amman. We had become refugees.

In retrospect, I am glad we did not witness the annihilation of our quarter. It turned out that a week after our departure, the Jewish holiday of Pentecost[7] was taking place, and Israelis in their hundreds of thousands gathered in front of the Wailing Wall, which stood just below our home. The house, naturally, was no longer there, just like the rest of the area. The entire neighborhood became one open space for the pilgrims. Gravel and dust were leveled on the remaining foundations, where houses, mosques, streets and squares had teemed with life just ten days earlier. For generations this used to be the Maghreb part of Jerusalem; now, no item of clothing, no piece of furniture, no single fig tree remained.

Meanwhile, for the Bargouti family in Bani Zeid, life was still bearable during the summer months. The Ramallah area was less damaged than many other places, and the occupation by the Israeli army did not seem, at first, detrimental to the future of the family. But soon confiscation warrants, restrictions and endless obstacles were imposed, hindering any normal life for them. Jewish settlements were established on all hilltops, and military jeeps crisscrossed the entire countryside. Like so many of the other young people Adnan, too, opted for a more secure life in Amman. He and I had to make do with our lot and tried to make the best of it. Both of us were enrolled in the Amman University for the '67–'68 year. We met each other anew and decided to build ourselves a future together. We got married in the summer of 1968, without our parents, without celebrations, without any special outfits.

As soon as Adnan reached Amman, he did not hesitate to join the Popular Front. He found work writing for the Front's *Al Shair Bulletin*, splitting his time between the university and the editorial office. The Popular Front advocated a democratic state for both Arabs and Jews. At the same time, it knew Israel would refuse to cede its independent status, and therefore the Front was determined to confront Israel militarily. It was arranged for us to spend the spring and summer months in Karameh, so that we could acquaint ourselves with the movement's routines. Adnan and I were planning to settle in an apartment in Amman in the autumn so that we could start a family. I had to request a year off university in order to give birth. All winter, I managed to continue my studies normally, but then in March, we were given a ride to Al Karameh.

Hearing about my family's experience in Jerusalem the previous year had strongly affected Adnan. He identified completely with our state of banishment and realized the nuclear part of the A-din family had disintegrated following the defeat. Our grandparents were in a refugee camp. My father, despite his heart condition, was obliged to search for work in Amman as a simple laborer. My parents moved from one rented room to another, unable to call anywhere home. I, myself, was lucky to have a place in the student dormitories.

Al Karameh

First and foremost, Karameh was about the view. The entire land of Palestine could be seen on the other bank of the Jordan River. Although from below the horizon was partially blocked by tall bulrushes and other swamp reeds, from above a vast landscape opened up. At times the fields adjacent to the river got covered by overflowing water and would teem with birds, frogs and fish. Adnan and I were happy. In a kind of a daze, we held hands, leaning back in traditional cane seats placed on the terrace. The setting sun was the backdrop to this perfect view.

Day broke early in Al Karameh. Most residents had a tight schedule of lessons and military exercises. Groups were seen practicing all around the village, and rifle ranges were situated by the cliffs or in the caves to its east. There weren't many of us there, perhaps one thousand people, mostly members of the liberation movement. Some farmers and shepherds lived among us, but they were a small minority. There prevailed a revolutionary atmosphere, one could say, of the intellectual kind. On the whole, residents were well-educated, many of them trained as engineers, pharmacists, teachers or physicians.

The Battle of March

Just days after our arrival at Al Karameh, and before we really settled into village life, the loathsome noise of engines I carried with me from the destruction of my home in Jerusalem returned: taking the place of the birds' chirping in the mornings was the sound of tank chains, revving armored vehicles and speeding jeeps. A helicopter showered information leaflets on Karameh, predicting evil. Just like the inhabitants of my Maghreb neighborhood, the inhabitants of Karameh were now ordered to evacuate before the destruction of the village. Most single men made their way up into the caves, while others took to their cars, dispersing in all directions. Adnan found it impossible to leave a pregnant wife on her own, but there seemed to be no vehicle available for me. Heavy bombardment could be heard in the distance before we could work out any plans; gunshots were exchanged not far from us. I could not stand the thought of once more abandoning the territory I inhabited, even though I well knew there was little chance of defending it against the army that only a year ago had captured so much land from Egypt, Syria and Jordan. Now it seemed that a new encounter between the Jordanian forces and the Israelis was taking place only kilometers away from us. Half an hour later, heavy fighting began between the Palestinians defending Al Karameh and the approaching Israelis, a battle taking the form of house-to-house skirmishes. We were about to take shelter in the municipal building, which had an underground basement, when jeeps encircled the courtyard, machine guns pointing at us. Adnan was immediately taken prisoner with other men his age. I had no idea where they were going. The few women remaining behind helped me down the stairs, but for the little ones inside me, it was too late. Painful convulsions took over me, and I was terrified I might give birth there and then. Once the pain ceased, a sort of numbness took its place. I lay on a mat, alongside cases of soda drinks and tins of fruit in syrup. I lost consciousness.

When I woke up, the village was still in the midst of fighting. I could hear helicopters as well as tank chains struggling uphill. Only many hours later, a medical physician examined me in the cellar and ordered my transfer to a hospital. Very few buildings were still standing, and the rest lay in heaps of rubble. The mosque and the municipal building stood in nearly a square kilometer of broken brick, cement blocks and stone. "Where was Adnan taken? Where is everyone?" I kept asking. An ambulance arrived from an Amman hospital. It seemed like a lifetime before I actually got there and proper test results came. I so wished that Adnan would appear all of a sudden by my side and that news of the babies' good health would be announced. This miracle never happened. Doctors informed me the pulse of one of the two fetuses had halted and that no details about the captured prisoners had been obtained. In my state, I could not return to the dormitories, and I remained in the hospital.

Victory

Crowds celebrated on the streets of Amman. From my hospital bed I could hear the honking of vehicles and the cheers of the intoxicated masses. On display were, apparently, Israeli army vehicles and ammunition taken as spoils. Jordanian troops marched the streets on parade. Interspersed with them were freedom fighters of various factions, each waving their corresponding flags. Gunshots celebrating the retreat of the Israeli army were heard all night. Was I imagining all this? Were bystanders making all sorts of stories up, just like the Syrian and Egyptian broadcasting radios, in the first days of June 1967, announcing a false triumph? I could not find out, and I could hardly care. I was losing endurance and stayed alive in the sole hope of finding Adnan again.

Weeks went by before I got to acknowledge the death of one of my children, a fetus I was still carrying together with his or her sibling. The heartbeat and movement of the surviving child gave me some courage. Two months into hospitalization, a message communicated by the Red Cross informed me that Adnan was imprisoned somewhere in the West

Bank. I was also told of scores of victims of the Karameh battle, both Israeli and Arab. At least Adnan was alive.

It is probably one of the worst human experiences to carry one's own dead child inside you. A part of me seemed to have died with the child, but the doctors refused to take any risks by removing it from the womb. The twins, dead and alive, remained inseparable.

Palestinians celebrated the birth of a popular movement for independence when I gave birth to Ramzi, the baby boy that survived. His sister, Feiza, was buried together with other Palestinian *shaids* in Al Karameh. In August 1968, Adnan was released in an exchange of prisoners. On the radio we heard the American ambassador to Israel admonishing the IDF for its complacency and the shadows the Karameh defeat cast on the Zionist dream. Regardless of everything, for us it was a new beginning.

An Erring Palestinian, a Wandering Jew or the Other Way Round

"Lame, I am lost on the edge of events, on the outskirts of things..."

The Blue Light, Hussein Barghouti.

In my mind I am conjuring up the son of the author Barghouti, himself conjuring the presence of his dad, since his father passed away when he was only two years old.

Father was nine when his mother traveled with him in an old Mercedes taxi, from Ramallah to the Allenby Bridge. At that period my grandfather worked in Lebanon, and during the long stretches of his absence, the family would join him there. This was no exile as in later years, yet for my father it was a foretaste of leaving home.

As the one-bedroom Beirut apartment was too small to accommodate them all, my future dad Hussein slept on a mattress by the entrance door. Late at night he was woken by the muezzin's call to prayer, and still in his pajamas he descended the narrow *kurkar* crags heading toward the beach. The boy Hussein recalled the Quran story of the sacrifice of Ismail. When he reached the bottom of the trail, sand replaced the *kurkar* gravel, and his bare feet indulged in the smooth and slightly warm sensation of the particles. Until that day he has not seen the sea, because in Palestine access to it was barred. He took off his nightwear and walked into the waves, expecting God to accept him just as he did Ismail in the anticipated sacrifice. Early in the morning, when his parents found Hussein on the beach, his mother could not stop crying.

My father's brother died when still very young and, according to tradition, was buried in a cave just outside town. For many years Father felt it was he that should have been sacrificed instead of the small dead brother, Salim. Perhaps, just like in the sacrifice story, the brothers were at times confused, alternately Isaac or Ismail attached to the altar. Instead, my father Hussein, when he reached the age of thirteen, was sent to a circumciser who peeled off and cut his foreskin without any disinfection or sedation. Perhaps because the pain was so great, my father could not even recall the event.

The hills and mountains surrounding Ramallah were bathed in sunlight a large part of the year, but during the winter months the freezing cold penetrated the stone walls. As Dad felt isolated already within his family and village, he began writing poems. Real barriers were added to mental ones, concrete checkpoints and automatic rifles cutting Ramallah off from the world. He read his poems to the family mule and the neighbors' sheep. When an alternative audience was sought, Hussein opted for exile. He had often heard that poets were revered in Eastern Europe. Hungary hovered at the edges of the Soviet Union and Europe, and the country was still licking the blood of its attempted independence. My father knew no Hungarian and still had a very limited vocabulary in English and French. Did he imagine himself reciting poetry in Arabic?

Although the Ottoman tiles of some of the bathhouses reminded him of his childhood mosques, he was now completely isolated. The Hungarian capital, with its many bridges, was to his liking, but it was also a city of drunkards and acrid workers. For the first time in his life, Father realized his terror not only of loneliness but also of losing his mind. Is it astonishing, then, that he had moved on from the homeless and alcoholics of a European metropolis to an American one, almost without taking notice of the displacement between continents? His friends were rambling addicts, mentally ill or drunks, but also retired hippies, retired prostitutes, and university students. How in the world was he able to complete a doctoral thesis when his nights were taken by idle meandering, by hours in smoky bars or in communes full of eccentrics?

For sure he wasn't your typical exile, but he was a wandering Palestinian. Father had acquired European culture and that of its younger sibling across the ocean from either elite, academic sources or from the most marginal and down-to-earth. Hussein would quote Aristotle, Schopenhauer, Hegel or T. S. Eliot as if they were the urchins of Wadi Adib. He mentioned classical composers from the Baroque period to the twentieth-century ones, and rap and punk bands of our own day. He was addicted to books, to cinema. Within twenty years he had digested the written, filmed, composed experience of the West, and in that respect, he became more Jewish than a Wandering Jew.

When Dad was quite ill, in place of a book about illness as a metaphor—a book someone else had already written—Hussein wished to write about exile as metaphor. But destiny had it he was exiled to another world, an exile of everlasting bliss.

The Head Administrator for the Territories

The chief administrator of the occupied territories would not go to bed without his Teddy bear. I repeat: the person responsible for all the daily details—from the right of a child to undergo leukemia therapy in the Hadassah Hospital, or a couple's right to marry, the bridegroom being from Jaffa while the bride is from Jenine, or a mathematician's right to go abroad for a conference—that person could not fall asleep at night nor take a nap at noontime without his Teddy.

Telling all this might not be all that acceptable legally or morally, what with respecting a person's privacy, or me bound by military secrecy while I was employed by the army, but now that I have been laid-off and tossed to the dogs, I don't really give a hoot.

At the time, I was working as a paid driver in the standing army. At first, I was assigned to the Head Educational Officer, whose base was in the center of the country, because I was newly married and we were expecting our first baby. But when we moved to Ma'aleh Edumim in the territories, I got a raise, and together with another driver we shared the accompaniment of the Chief Civil Administrator, using a brand-new Ford Escort. Don't ask me why the official title of the man was *Chief Civil Administrator* when it was universally obvious he was a military officer, and that I, myself, was in uniform. The man was answerable to the Minister of Defense, after all...but certain things are simply beyond me.

At any event, N.N. got driven to all corners of the occupied territories, as well as those within the Green Line.[8] Among other places, I would drive him to a weekly appointment with a psychologist. Of course, I was not meant to know that it was a psychologist's office, but after a year of chauffeuring and as a result of certain developments, I probably heard and overheard things that I was not meant to. And yes, it could also be said I gained the confidence of N.N. to a degree that put him as a private but also professional person in jeopardy.

To be honest, right from the beginning I felt something was odd with N.N. Not for a second do I mean to suggest that he wasn't polite or considerate with me. On the contrary, I have never had a more considerate boss than him. But still, it was awkward to be driving together, neither of us uttering a sound, but him bursting into a nervous laugh all of a sudden, as if some funny joke had just been told. A second later, he was his normal serious self again. N.N. was not married and, as far as I know, was not dating anyone. For a time I thought this might be the problem, and I suggested he join public singing sessions held near his home, or that he benefit from free tickets to concerts and other events, tickets I was entitled to through my association with my former boss at the Entertainment and Education army sector. But all this was of no interest to him. Several times I invited him to my home, but he came only once, on New Year's Eve, to wish my wife a sweet and happy new year. Ten minutes later, N.N. requested that I drive him back home.

He had all kinds of ideas in mind—*projects*, as he called them—related mostly to the occupied territories, to Arabs, and that kind of thing. Original ideas, I must add. This was probably the reason N.N. had to give up his job and take early retirement or, as he called it, *voluntary departure*, due to exhaustion.

One has to admit, he might have had a point there: N.N. had some issue around falling asleep. If during a ride, seated next to me or in the back, he would unintentionally fall asleep, he would wake up in fright, and in the mirror or peripherally I would catch a look of dread, as if I was the angel of death in person, or at least a blood-thirsty Arab. N.N. had a thing about Arabs, which I could not quite fathom. It is not as if I personally like Arabs or anything, but he had a real fear of them. This was the reason, I think, he got to know Arabic so well: at all costs N.N. wanted to know what they were saying or, better still, what they were thinking. My own Arabic was sufficient for buying cigarettes or Turkish Delight; that was all I needed. The last thing I wished was to know what Arabs were thinking. Who at all cares? N.N.'s most ambitious project was the creation of an alternative Palestinian leadership. He felt that puppet leaders installed in the occupied territories could do our job, taking all the risks upon themselves. They would know, though, that if they did not remain loyal to us, we would just replace them with other puppets. For some reason, higher grades—the Ministry of Defense, the General Staff or what have you—did not take to the idea. I personally found it quite cool.

The other issue was even less obvious, and here the psychologist's appointments come into the picture. One day, completely out of the blue, without me inquiring or anything, N.N. told me that these unofficial get-togethers in the Tel Aviv area—the very appointments I was not meant to know about—were in fact gatherings intended to prepare soldiers for psychological warfare or, more precisely, psychological self-defense in facing the Arabs. N.N. would usually use the term *locals*. On another occasion, I remember him leaving some staff meeting muttering, but at the same time lecturing to himself, "How could one mistake them for human beings, like you and me? If originally they resembled us, now that we rule over them, they cease being like us...This has to be explained to the soldiers. One has to prepare them. They need to understand the psychology of the locals. Yes, yes, our duty as officers is to analyze to the smallest detail, their psychology. This is our task right now..."

Once, after one of N.N.'s weekly appointments near Tel Aviv, he told me upon leaving, "This time we have really managed to define the prototype of a local resident of the territories, the typical local. I need to encounter the best psychologists in order to come up with such a model."

On another occasion, when I came to fetch him from the psychologist's office, I had to wait a long time. I thought he might have left with someone else, neglecting to call me. I went in to find out. What stopped me, a meter away from the office door, was the sound of crying or, better said, sobbing: sobs like those of a young, abandoned child. I recognized N.N.'s voice. Immediately, I returned to the Ford Escort as if I had not heard a thing. But obviously I began asking myself some questions. Following that, it became clear to me that no *prototype* or whatever was at stake and that other issues altogether were being brought up in that office. Soon enough, I had, in fact, the confirmation that the office was a psychologist's clinic. I don't mean to be boasting or something: one did not require a detective in order to figure it out, just have some basic common sense... Dropping N.N. off for one of those appointments, I bumped into an old friend of my sister's. She couldn't talk to me straightaway as she first had to pick up a jacket she had left behind. Seconds later, apologizing, she returned with the jacket, stepping out of the very door N.N. had entered earlier. I inquired whether she had some dealings with the army nowadays, still thinking the office was requisitioned for military use. My sister's friend had to laugh in embarrassment: just an ordinary psychologist's office, she said. Finding herself in the middle of a complicated divorce, she explained, she felt the need for some counseling. I restrained myself and did not mention anything about my boss.

Later came a period during which N.N., instead of chuckling for no apparent reason, would cry in the car. Upon the second time it happened, I realized something deep inside had gone wrong with him. Strangely, this was also the period he was most excited about the so-called prototype business and elaborated on the subject to me, or to himself, but in my presence.

"Soldiers ought to exercise indifference to the emotions of locals, especially when children, women or the elderly are concerned. Crying or whimpering do not indicate necessarily a state of suffering. In half of the cases, it is merely a staged display of emotions. When journalists are present, it is safe to say that eighty percent of the locals' behavior is faked. Naturally, it is not easy to empty a house of its inhabitants in the middle of the night and then proceed to destroy the home. The task must be made easier for the soldiers, as it is not obvious for them that a house can represent a security risk or that a village needs to be collectively punished. Psychologists must install resilience in soldiers and help them control their emotions."

N.N. even spoke of techniques developed for separating babies from the clutches of their mums, on using infants and toddlers to entice their parents out of a home. He had theories about everything, and it drove me nuts to hear him lecture like this, in an intellectual manner and tone of voice.

The day I found out about the Teddy, it was raining heavily, and long traffic jams formed around the Ge'ha junction. We weren't totally stuck, but cars were moving at a crawl. N.N. had decided we had better stop for supper, even though it was just past five p.m. Because of the rain and the early sunset, I tried parking the Escort as close to the restaurant as possible, leaving it partially on the sidewalk. Half an hour later, returning from the restaurant, the car was no longer there. Cheech[9] or some other municipal officials (enthusiasts of car-towing) decided to show off their efficiency exactly on a wet day like today," I said in frustration. "Didn't they notice, for heaven's sake, that ours was a military car?"

N.N. sank into a sort of trance and hardly reacted. With his arm, he steadied himself against a low, wet wall in front of the restaurant, staring at the spot where the Escort had been parked.

"I'll call headquarters for another vehicle," I told him. "There is no point standing out here in the rain. Go inside for a second cup of hot tea, and I will join you for one, in a moment."

"It is my bag," N.N. said faintly, "the bag was left in the car..."

"No worries," I said, "your papers and documents are in the cardboard folder you've got with you. In the car you only had spare overnight belongings. We'll get the bag back, as soon as the Escort is released."

"It might take all night," he said in a kind of desperation. "I cannot possibly spend the night without the bag."

N.N. had cracked. To him it was the end of the world. He kept giving the restaurant's lamppost, which had meanwhile lit up, short but fierce strikes with his shoe. He kicked and wept bitterly at the same time. In the yellow light of it, his face appeared like a Japanese mask, in a sort of twitch of pain.

Once a driver arrived with a substitute vehicle, N.N. was somewhat calmer but still insisted on being brought to the psychologist's office. After about fifteen minutes of waiting for N.N., the psychologist himself came out to let us know we were free for the night, that N.N. would arrange to return home on his own.

The following morning I checked out the Ford Escort from the municipal towed-cars lot. N.N.'s bag was lying on the back seat, as on the previous evening. Still, I wanted to make sure nothing was stolen from it and, in an automatic move, opened the bag for confirmation. There was a neatly folded pair of pajamas, a spare pair of socks and underwear, toothpaste and brush, and a medium-size Teddy bear, well-worn but standing as if on guard, like a soldier, next to the personal belongings.

Slightly later than usual, I collected N.N. from his apartment, but not a word was said either about the car or the Teddy bear or the events of the previous night.

How an Average Left-winger Ends Up in a Colony of the Far Right?

Having spent years in Europe, the thought of doing reserve military service in Israel had become alien to me. My parents went abroad frequently, allowing family reunions to take place away from Israel, and even among natives of that country the weight of such a duty seemed to have dwindled with time. Which is why the Notice No. 80 that awaited me at my parents' home when I arrived there for their fiftieth wedding anniversary was such a surprise. I thought I'd be able to get the issue resolved, exchanging a few words with the coordination office in Tel Aviv. The Kafkaesque reality, though, had a logic all its own. A female top sergeant, with brightly painted fingernails, explained to me that residence in foreign countries did not exempt one from duties toward one's homeland. On the contrary, according to her, during my years abroad I contributed little to the safety of my country, or my parents for that matter. A visit to Israel was, therefore, an opportunity to pay back such a debt. My return airline ticket, to be used a few days later, did not duly impress the sergeant. According to her, military service justified the modifying of travel arrangements. In fact, the law enabled the army to recruit me for a number of weeks, but since the top sergeant facing me was an understanding person who took my age into consideration—which was nearly forty—she would limit the present reserve military duty to a tiny, wee week.

The question that pulsed in my head like a pneumatic drill was why in the world I hadn't forgone my Israeli nationality and contented myself with European papers. The reply to such a simple interrogation was complicated, or illogical, like so many other issues. Following the Holocaust, one could not overlook one's attachment to a Jewish State. As long as my parents were still living in Israel, and taking into account the role Israel had played in saving their lives when they arrived as European refugees, I necessarily had mixed feelings about that place.

I was sent, as a guard, to one of the most politically extreme communities in the West Bank: the colony of Even Bahir. It entered my mind, of course, that I could plainly refuse the order, just as I had done during my three years of ordinary military service and on a number of additional occasions, when I had felt strong enough to face incarceration. There was a chance it would work this time around as well. But there were equal chances I would have to spend a number of weeks in army detention and be ordered to complete my week's worth of reserve service afterward. I had a feeling, taking into consideration my previous reputation in the army, that the whole week was invented, as it were, to test my resistance and remind me what my proper place was. Another possible explanation to this sudden *call to arms* was the expansion of colonies in the occupied territories and the lack of military personnel to protect the settlers.

The day-to-day routine of the occupation was a shock to a softy like myself, pampered by an easy life in Europe. On either left or right, military vehicles in high gear doubled the civilian cars, especially where local Palestinian licensed ones were concerned. Road checkpoints slowed down the traffic every ten kilometers or so, each time sorting out the supposed bad guys from the good, according to license plates, identification cards and physical features. The Israeli apartheid functioned efficiently as usual, the way it had since...since how long, exactly? The illusion something was changing, each time a new treaty was signed or other circumstances changed, was exactly that: an illusion. The domination of a conquered population has sunk its roots, deeper and deeper, not just since I was born but way before that. In the corner of an army jeep, hoping to become invisible, I squeezed my 1.80 meters into as little space as possible. Fewer and fewer cars were visible after the Arab town of Jit and the junction bypassing Nablus. The surrounding view seemed to be taken out of an engraving book, possibly the impressions of an eighteenth-century European explorer. Mountain stone terraces, flocks of sheep and olive trees spread all the way to the horizon. Only on the hilltops, ambitious building projects, crowned with antennas and solar panels, formed a clear contrast: the colonies.

Forking off the main road on the right, the jeep advanced to the barbed-wire fence and control barrier of the settlement Even Bahir. A tinny voice in the walkie-talkie requested Dudi, head of security. As if responding to the wave of a magic wand, a Quad appeared on the other side of the fence, carrying full-geared Dudi: an M16, and a loaded pistol hung on each side of him while side curls and the four corners of his fringed garment were waving in the wind.

This is how my week-long, robot like existence in a colony of the Far Right commenced. A week during which I tried hard to refrain from entering any debate or dispute, avoiding, if at all possible, even the act of contemplation or doubt. My sole and profound wish was to survive seven days without having to kill a person. At dusk, following five straight hours of controlling cars and vans, identification documents and delivery papers, and just before the night guard came to replace me, Rosie Levie showed up at the barrier.

Did I know any French? she inquired, before even presenting herself or saying *hello*. In my mind I would have recalled as a clever literary association *The Little Prince* with his request for a drawing of a sheep, had there not been security cameras, blade wires and an Israel armed to its teeth all around me.

"Yes, I do," I replied, and the soundtrack that would accompany me for the next few days began rolling, in a pleasant if somewhat piping voice.

Rose and her husband Jacques (Jacob) had moved to Even Bahir from France two years earlier. She had not overcome the language barrier and had to content herself with, at most, four or five sentences in Hebrew. The couple was only a few years my senior but already had daughters aged eighteen and nineteen. The entire family walked around armed, and Jacques had a loaded semiautomatic rifle by his bed at night. Even the Yeshiva student they hosted as a paid guest had a pistol, despite his debilitating Tourette's syndrome, with its involuntary brisk movements and incoherent cries. He occasionally threw up an arm or even both arms in the air, calling out a muffled phrase. I was invited to their house, first for cookies and lemonade, and a few days later for the Shavu'ot (Pentecost) eve get-together. On Friday evening, there followed a Shabbat prayer and meal. It turned out Rosie's need to speak French was stronger than any timetable or other obliging factors. On my part, I did nothing to encourage these invitations or conversations. As I have already said, I merely hoped to get through the week alive.

The daymare began early the next day, the second of Sivan, the year 5765, according to the traditional Jewish calendar (a tradition assigned to Hillel II, I was told, an offspring of Rabbi Yehuda, the president of Sanhedrin). Vans and minibuses appertaining to settlements called Kalila, Bat Kol, Khoshen or Barak arrived at the colony gate at eight a.m. They were transporting children and teens that presented, I felt, a danger to public order, even without carrying any sort of arms. Since I wasn't wearing a skullcap and was there supposedly to render them a service, straightaway they nicknamed me the Shabbat Goy.[10] The skullcaps worn by the boys arriving for the Even Bahir day camp had short slogans woven into their cotton yarmulkes, such as *Messiah Now* or *Bibi for the Jews*. The girls wore mostly long skirts, with their hair covered or fastened in the back. When the youngsters inside the vehicles felt I was too slow in opening the gate or verifying documents, a chain of nasty expressions and swearwords was called out at me from the open windows. The van drivers, almost all unfortunate hired day laborers, did little to reproach the kids, when it wasn't they themselves who were uttering the abuse.

Rosie kept me up-to-date concerning the day-camp activities of the children, her eldest daughter being one of its counselors, and Rosie herself taking an active part in it. The girls, six to sixteen, spent mornings in beautification and personal care workshops, with homemaking, literature and Zionism left for the afternoons. Rosie, as the hairdresser of Even Bahir, hosted some fifty girls under her hair-drying helmet during the week of activities, using a collection of photos to determine the desired hairdo. She relied heavily on hand gestures, calling out in her strident voice, French terms, such as *franges ,coupe* or *permanente*. Her daughter, as the person coordinating the beautification activity, was around for some translations when called for. The boys, on the other hand, at least those aged ten and up, received basic instruction in handling weapons and maintaining and operating guns and pistols. Even a semiautomatic rifle made the rounds of the workshop—luckily unloaded. Afternoon activities for the youngsters included hand-grenade and Molotov-cocktail training, using simulated substitutes, perhaps due to some shortage.

Driven off each evening, the youth seemed to me not only content and excited but even exhilarated and hot-tempered. *Arabs out, don't mess about* or *Rabin, bloody traitor* were some of the calls they were enthusiastically chanting. That very evening, in Rosie and Jacques's home, I found out that the phrases exclaimed by their Yeshiva guest during a Tourette's fit were, in fact, in total contrast to the slogans called out by the day-camp teens. "Germany was fun," he would mutter or "Let's return to Treblinka." Where in the world did he come across such content? No one had the slightest idea. Even the Yeshiva student himself seemed all confused when asked about it.

Prior to Shavuot day, the frenzy inhabited not just the youngsters but the entire settlement of Even Bahir. Awkwardly, I felt happy to be posted at the entrance of the colony, despite the humiliating calls and the disdain, thinking that perhaps this way other potential victims might be spared, at least to a degree, the rage of the fiery children. These might have been some isolated Arab women on the side of the road, an elderly person at the entrance of Nablus or some poor shepherds. The teens' cry *Rabin, bloody traitor* permitted me to guess their view of someone like me. A secular Jew from the center of Israel was not very different in their eyes from an Arab. The only element that established a certain distance, and a form of respect—although the word *respect* in this context is probably inappropriate—was perhaps the fact that I carried a gun. I knew, ironically, that the youths' acquaintance and experience with weapons was probably twice that of my own and that, surely, their eagerness to make use of a gun was some ten times greater. In what situation, I asked myself, would I actually feel ready to make use of my weapon, or what amount of force would I exert to prevent some of these kids, or someone else, from stealing the gun from me?

Strange people frequented the settlement barrier during the evening time, when the community returned to a quiet existence at the end of a day of furor. Like Rosie, there were other new immigrants that found Hebrew difficult: Russians, Americans and South Americans. There were a few families of Ethiopian origin, and they, too, had some language problems or other difficulties integrating. One or two women supplied me with water or sandwiches from time to time. This is how I got to know other residents of Even Bahir. Out of boredom, one older person, traveling around in his electric chair, would stop by to say *hello* once or twice a day. An Ethiopian boy of about twelve frequently walked along the fence, like an animal in a cage. He completely ignored his parents and other adults, who would tell him it was forbidden and dangerous to do that. Unlike the women who offered me water, the boy would come to me instead, asking for a drink. Rosie, though, remained my main visitor and host. There were no incidents I had to report to her, other than occasional shots and explosions that were to be heard in the distance. These originated, apparently, from shooting ranges in adjacent valleys, exercises by either Jewish or Palestinian groups. The explosions originated, more often than not, from construction sites where dynamite was used in the cracking of rocks before the laying of building foundations. As a simple reserve soldier, I wasn't meant to pay any attention to such details, but I was sure learning things.

Matan Torah, or the reception of the Book of Books, a holiday that coincided with shavu'ot, was the climax of that particular week. What degree of exhilaration could still be expected? I was wondering. Would the Messiah suddenly appear? Would the erection of the Third Temple commence? Rosie made sure I remained on firmer ground, complaining to me about suburban hostilities back in cities such as Toulouse or Marseilles, initiated mostly by immigrants from North Africa, according to her, and often followed by attacks on Jewish synagogues or schools. "We did not wish our grandchildren to be raised in that sort of climate," Rosie was telling me. "We should have moved to Netanya or Holon, but we just did not have that kind of money. At least here, in the territories, we are the ones in control, not *them*."

"For better or worse," Jacques added, he who usually refrained from contributing to the conversation. And in biblical Hebrew he mumbled,

"In the heart of the Shomron."

At the end of a week's military duty, a week that seemed the product of some sick and delirious mind, I returned to the center of the country. Assuming the same fetus position, I hid myself in the back seat of a public bus, since no military transport was available that day. Some other reserve soldiers and quite a few settlers were making use of the same interurban line. Among them, I felt guilty, embarrassed and outraged all at the same time, like some puppy that has wet himself and then in addition gets scolded by his owner. Don't ask me why I came up with this pathetic simile. Probably just exhaustion.

All that was left for me to do was iron some of the clothes that went through the washing machine and dryer, then pack for my flight back home the following day. Photographs of my parents' fiftieth wedding anniversary were tossed in a side pocket of the suitcase, together with small bags of spices, crisp soup lentils and pistachios—all seeming like some shipwreck relics from a vessel, stranded in the middle of the Mediterranean.

The Amir Family

At first I envisaged a title such as Kibbutz Holland or even Kibbutz Amsterdam but feared it would raise the wrong expectations or even attract the wrong crowd, one eager for sexual anecdotes about foreign volunteers, especially female ones, to Israeli kibbutzim—a sort of amalgam between the Red District in Amsterdam, which almost every tourist is drawn to, and cohabitation habits of kibbutz members. So very little is commonly known about private life in kibbutz communities that a sort of halo of secrecy had grown around the subject, partly due to the fact only some three percent of the Israeli population live in such social structures. As a result, fantasies were quite common, especially in the 1960s and 70s, concerning what went on beyond the walls of tiny kibbutz homes, on the part of a variety of groups, Zionist or non-Zionist, Jews or Gentiles. Rumors spread so wildly, that it felt at some point that the kibbutz concept was invented more for those daydreamers than for the few individuals that actually lived there. But to me, this present tale isn't just about sexual fantasies. It might sound pompous or pretentious, expecting a few pages to capture the identity of a whole generation of kibbutz dwellers or to convey the entire phenomenon of Kibbutz volunteers in one story, but this was always my problem. From a very young age, I felt existence had a kind of a code that could be deciphered. Once, aged seventeen or so, I was attempting to describe to my dad this very conviction of mine. He was driving me to a meeting in Tel Aviv, concerning, incidentally, the objectives of a *Nahal*[11]initiative to support various kibbutzim in the Galilee. (I was never a kibbutz member myself, but being part of a *Nahal* kibbutz group was as near as I got to being one.) I went on and on about the potential of a certain image or a formula to contain the truth of an entire event. The car was already parked at my destination as I continued my theory. Finally all my father could say about my rambling was "Now get out of the car."

The story begins in 1949 and spans some sixty years to the present day, at least for the time being. 1949 was the year of the birth of Asaf Amir (short form, *Asi*), as well as that of Liesbeth (*Betty*) Amir, née van Huizen. Asi was born in kibbutz Kfar Yehuda (the name invented for the sake of the story), situated in the north of the Negev desert, to parents of Hungarian origin. There, in the children's home of the kibbutz, Asi learned that his very childhood was the realization of the Zionist ideal. And in fact, it was at times quite taxing living together with eleven more children, in two elongated halls, instead of spending his childhood in his parents' own home as their only son. Separating every day was the hardest part, perhaps, as at six o'clock in the evening one had to detach oneself from one's parents, grandparents, neighbors and friends after spending only two or three hours with them. At six Asi had to pick up his towel from the hallway, where name tags of all twelve children were posted on the wall, just above twelve hooks, recoup his bar of soap with its plastic container from the cubby, also labeled with his name, undress and hang his clothes above the cubby. Then, all five boys and seven girls of his group entered the shower room.

Asi recounts: "My earliest memory is of the children's wagon, in which three other toddlers stood staring, just like me. Our group, the *Hatsav* (squill) group, had three more similar wagons, unlike the *Rakefet* (cyclamen) group, the older children of the home, which had only two wagons. On every outing—named *tiyul*, as if we were on a hike—three sturdy women pushed our wagons through the kibbutz paths. These were our foster moms, one could say. The walk to and from the laundry room was for us an exploration of the outside world: the adults' dining hall, the library (which served also as a culture club, with a real turntable and vinyl records), the grocery distribution room and finally the laundry. There, every few days we collected towels, sheets and clean clothes and deposited our soiled articles. All these were shared items for all kibbutz members, and none carried any personal names. Clothes were just distributed according to size. I joined my parents after our afternoon nap.

"For my mother and grandma, saying good-bye toward evening time was like catching the last train before the Nazis' invasion, a drama played over and over again, everyday. My parents narrowly escaped Hungary before it was too late. For me and my father, it became a family joke when I turned older, as the organization of groups departing for Palestine, during the war, was coded in Hebrew *tiyul*, just like my own childhood outings. I personally would not have minded so much the farewell hour had it not been for my mother's tears. On the other hand, I felt grown-up when my father kept repeating, 'Our son is already resilient by now.' It sounded like a military award or something."

The father of Asi, Yitshak Amir, was one of the founders of Kfar Yehuda and back in Hungary had organized a cell of the Zionist youth movement. Instead of pursuing a career as an attorney, he had chosen to emigrate with a group of young Jews, which included, incidentally, Asi's future mother. Back in Hungary, they were called Isaac and Elna Ulman. Deep inside, they were not convinced socialists, but the idea they must overcome their own needs in order to forward the collective cause—in what seemed a total sacrifice of themselves—suited them well at the time. Without entering lengthy discussions and exchanging very few words even between themselves, they contributed actively to the development of their small community. Compared to the Hungarian capital and even to the Pest ghetto in the middle of it, the city of Be'er Sheva seemed like a mere metro station. Kfar Yehuda was just a lost spot in the middle of the Negev desert: ten huts and a similar number of tents, borrowed or stolen from the British army. To reach Palestine in the 1940s, they had to use forged identity and travel documents. Certain members of the Hungarian Zionist movement managed to obtain Hungarian army uniforms and even outfits of fascist unions, pretending to escort the escaping Jews to imaginary detention centers. In 1949, when Asi was born, the State of Israel was one year old. Only then did it seem legitimate to Elna and Isaac, to bear a child. Back then, few in the kibbutz knew of their newly adopted Hebrew names. It was still awkward, even for them, to be called the Amir family, when waiting in line at the health clinic or when receiving official mail. Elna became Ilana and Isaac became Yitshak.

Asi: "More than anything else, even more than the common showers or the dormitory, what bugged me most was sharing a meal in the children's home. There was no one to back me, saying, 'Just leave the bread crusts on the side of your plate, it's not a big deal' or 'The vegetables can wait for another time.' Our chaperones in the children's home obliged us to eat up everything. It must be recalled that I grew up during the Tsena restrictions period and that food was limited. A group of twelve children like ours, for example, had to share one chocolate bar and even that only two or three times a week. Perhaps a genetic heritage or something made fresh vegetables indigestible to me. I could only stand well-cooked vegetables, more in line with the East European tradition. All that was hard or leafy I literally detested. Even pieces of apricot mixed in yogurt would get stuck in my throat and make me want to throw up. This drove the head child-carer, Khayuta, up the wall. For her, it was pure provocation, or even a sign of bourgeois resistance. You may imagine what a nightmare this turned into. I remained a small and skinny child, even though my parents did their best to compensate for the horror I was facing by occasionally offering me a bowl of soup in which meat and vegetables were ground to paste or even a cupcake filled with cream. To this very day I cannot eat fresh fruit and vegetables that haven't been peeled first. Red or green peppers were, and still are, off my list of edibles, and so it was my luck that they became the kibbutz's prized product. You may find Kfar Yehuda peppers in supermarkets all over Europe."

In 1960,Khayuta's group, Khatsav, moved to a new building. Asi was old enough to walk to and from his parents' home on his own, or with his friend Oded whose parents lived in the same group of houses. They would discuss the fact Na'ama, a girl from their group—slightly disabled mentally but physically more advanced than her peers—was now taking her showers separately from their group. Oded claimed she already had pubic hair. At the end of that year, two other girls moved up to the Rakefet group, apparently for similar reasons.

Asi: "At that time, I began not only paying closer attention to what was happening around me, little details concerning the behavior or the development of the children in Khatsav, but keeping track of things that caught my eye, sketches or lists of events all noted down in an old schedule book, used in the past for planning work shifts in the kibbutz. It had thick, rough pages and a cardboard cover: in a word, it was perfect for my needs. I attributed code names to people and used code words, in case someone came across the notes. On one of the opening pages there was a rudimentary sketch of a woman/girl, washing in a tin tub. I don't know where I got the idea for the tub, maybe from the laundry room. In our groups no such tubs were in use, I don't think. Although no title is given, it probably depicted Na'ama. I drew stubble between her legs.

"While the bodies of all other children of the group were changing, I myself had to wait in misery till the age of fourteen for my body to develop. In order to answer so many questions I struggled with, the sketches, caricatures and, later on, the Czech Meopta camera I received as a gift became an essential part of my life. The foundations for my later career as a photographer are to be found in those years. To me, the pencil or the camera was a formidable weapon. My perspective and priorities changed drastically in those days. I was now eager to return every day to the children's group from my parents' small apartment. Up to a certain point, my collection of flint arrowheads, empty bullet cartridges and even a discarded bombshell, leftover from the 1956 conflict—all those objects displayed above a guest bed in my parents' abode—evoked and implied a mature and virile self-identity. Now, all of a sudden, when the children around me were all turning into adolescents, I felt like a tiny gnome left behind in the garden. It became like an obsession for me, to try and get rid of a sense of vulnerability, the helplessness of a naked child, faced with a changing reality."

And the world was indeed changing fast around Asi. In 1962, Nasser nationalized half of the industry and commerce in Egypt, siding with Khrushchev's Soviet Union to create, more or less, the Middle East we know of today: the US with its Eastern and Western allies, against a smaller number of Russian-aligned countries. The old colonial makeup had been shaken, China had its cultural revolution, and a major nuclear confrontation was closely avoided in Cuba. Only by the end of that year did Asi's body catch up with the ticking clock of his age group. Pubic hair appeared at the bottom of his belly, millimeters above his testicles and penis, they, too, slowly joining the local revolution. Unlike the rest of the Khatsav group, Asi refused to learn the Bible portion to be read as part of his bar mitzvah birthday and decided to invent his own coming-of-age rite. Together with Dani, a friend from the Rakefet group (Oded meanwhile had moved to Ashdod, his father employed by the municipal authorities in constructing the new port), he planned to smuggle himself across the Jordanian border. To the boys, Petra's Red Rock suggested itself as the ultimate destination for an initiation journey. When they realized Petra was beyond their capabilities, the second-best site was agreed upon: Masada. On August 3, 1963, the two boys reach Be'er Sheva in order to join a Boy Scouts' trip to Arad. On that date the national scout movement held its annual Jamboree and, exceptionally, Asi and Dani were allowed to take part, even though they weren't regular members. The boys' plan was to escape the Scouts' camp during the night, walk through Wadi Morag, an arid riverbed, to reach another trail in Wadi Ye'elim. They wanted to hide during the day and attempt the climb of the ancient fortified plateau Masada early the next morning. Things got complicated when they immediately lost their way on the first night. While older Scouts were holding a clandestine makeup session, decorating the faces of the sleeping younger Scouts, they come across the empty tent of Asi and Dani. The Arad police were alerted, and after an hour or two of joint efforts by police and Scouts, the boys were found in a valley branching off Wadi Morag. An old Bedouin living there with his skinny goats let Asi and Dani spend the night in the camel-hair tent. The following day both boys were accompanied back to their kibbutz.

Asi: "A whole assortment of newspaper clips and photos made it to my scrapbook—images were not easy to come by, in those days. I would cut out pictures from magazines, such as the one of dead Egyptian infiltrators who had crossed the border near Beit Govrin. In 1963, we got to watch the movie *Lawrence of Arabia* in a real Be'er Sheva cinema. Of course, we were highly impressed. Few films were shown in the kibbutz, and mostly they were damaged copies projected onto a white bed sheet in the dining hall. I sacredly removed a publicity picture of Peter O'Toole from a newspaper of that period. With some imagination, one could see him as an Israeli undercover agent.

"When I was still a teenager, foreign volunteers began arriving at the kibbutz. Of course, not quite the numbers we had after 1967, but still. All kinds of anthropologists and sociologists made it to Kfar Yehuda as well, examining how and what exactly was going on, theories, sometimes completely crackpot, appearing in scientific journals. I had my own speculation about volunteers in the kibbutz. Perhaps someone else had already come up with the same idea meanwhile, I don't know. In my mind, the phenomenon began because the kibbutz was such a hermetically closed society, in which sexual relations were a taboo, like within a family. With all the tensions, especially after the sixties' revolutions, women's liberation, the pill, and the colorful hippies, the sexual energy just had to go somewhere. With the arrival of the volunteers from the outside world, especially female volunteers from the Netherlands or from Scandinavia, a whole generation of kibbutz children was born with blond hair. No miracles or anything. This, too, calls for no sociologists or statisticians to be proven right."

All sorts of explanations exist to analyze the phenomenon of kibbutz volunteers: financial, political, social. But Asi's point of view is interesting, nevertheless. After 1967, Israel was daily in the news, and interest in communal living and the East increased, especially in Europe and the United States. Airplane tickets became cheaper, and soon Israel turned into a tourist destination. The issue of societal morals is worth looking at, but prior to that, one mustn't forget that 1967 was, first and foremost, the year of the war. The Israeli–Arab conflict took a sharp turn and became almost irreversible.

Asi: "It was no longer necessary for me to invent my own initiation ceremonies in 1967: an accelerated military training had sent me directly to my baptism by fire. By then, I had surpassed the standard 1.60 meters in height. It seemed natural that I remain in the south of Israel, an area I got to know quite well, and so I joined the combat unit Shaked. Being an only child allowed me some privileges, and my mother nudged me to request a clerical position in Intelligence. But she knew right from the beginning that I would pay little attention to that, like to many other of her wishes. She was even criticized by some kibbutz members who claimed there was no such thing as a single child in a children's home. It was still a comfort to her that I was stationed close by so that on military leave, home visits were made easier.

"Nowadays, the American army encourages its recruits to look up icons such as Lawrence of Arabia before leaving on a mission to Iraq, for example. We, here in Israel, had our own historical figures to study, such as Orde Wingate. His hit-brigade tactics were explained in military prep schools. In the Negev, our inspiration came sometimes from unexpected sources. Desert-agricultural techniques, for example, enabled us to plow the area parallel to the border fence in order to detect any footprints or other suspect traces or marks from a potential enemy. The Shaked had a theoretical instruction section of its own, with maps, charts and markers in all colors. Which brings me to my own first military ingenuity that was applauded, but much less heroic. Lacking colored fabrics to highlight our pinned unit emblems, I just stripped the billiards table in the Egyptian officers' club in Sharem-a Sheikh. It had the green felt perfect for our purposes. Improvisation due to a low budget or lack of time became our mode of functioning, our motto being *Don't put off till tomorrow what you are able to achieve today*.

"The first casualty of the 1967 war was probably an Israeli pilot shot down by my friend Dani, from Kfar Yehuda. For the rest of his life, he could not forgive himself for that mistake, but orders were orders: shoot down any aircraft approaching Dimona, he was told. The risk that the nuclear site, operational only for a year or two, would be targeted was too high. One of the psychological advances we had in 1967 was that the napalm bomb was there, in case everything else failed. I won't get into the details of the first week of the war, but our unit, Shaked, lost soldiers and even officers. The damage we caused Egypt was not particularly pretty either. But at the end of that week, I turned into a man. There was no looking back. The Asi you see in front of you today, losing hair and going all wrinkled, is the same Asi I turned into during that war. Every get-together of Shaked ex-soldiers, or even a casual encounter in, say, Amsterdam or downtown Tel Aviv, is for us a moment when time stands still."

Six years later, when Liesbeth arrived at kibbutz Kfar Yehuda, Asi is already past his second war, a mature man, despite the fact his life's dream—a dream suppressed and almost secret—had not yet materialized. A black diary had taken the place of his old scrapbook, in which he continued drawing or jotting down highlights and the curiosities of his life. Regarding his interaction with girls, for example, he wrote that he had some emotional involvement with students from the regional high school of Sha'ar Hanegev but that his sexual initiation did not come until his return from three years of military service.

In accordance with his theory about volunteers, this experience was indeed with a German volunteer, a girl a few years his senior, who on the surface seemed very serious and lacking any erotic aspirations. That he could freely stare at Ingrid's naked body without concealing the fact from anyone else was for Asi the thing that moved him the most. In his room, he would point the reading lamp right up against Ingrid's soft skin and get excited by every square centimeter of it. To Asi's surprise, the skin was far from being all smooth, but like the grains of dune sand found all over the Negev, it was rich in minute details. Every corner was worth exploring. Here was a patch of blond feathery down, there a tiny birthmark. Ingrid's breasts were a live and vibrant world of their own. More than any other part of her body, the simile Asi drew between the desert dunes and the human being was obvious in Ingrid's chest. Light played games on the surface, as if the sun was shining on the desert through autumn clouds. The discharge at the end of the journey was like rainfall after a long summer month. Each time, Asi felt anew that the long wait, all those years that he withheld himself sexually, had now paid off.

Apart from some weeks replacing the kibbutz administrator and, of course, the weeks he was on reserve military duties, Asi spent all his time working as a dairyperson, in the Kfar Yehuda cowshed. In 1973, his reserve service coincided, as for so many other Israeli men, with the October War. This, for Asi, also involved a car accident with the military Susita he was driving that ended up a total loss. As a result, he spent more time in the hospital than on the battlefield. Apart from the fact Israel was *caught with its trousers down*, as Asi puts it, for him 1967–1973 seemed almost like one continuous war, with him taking the years of Attrition fighting along the Suez Canal into account. The exception was, he is quick to add, that the number of casualties in that wretched month of October was hundredfold.

During these six years, casual relationships with women alternated for Asi, as volunteers to the kibbutz came and left. As part of their exploration of communal living, Middle-Eastern food and exotic Egged-company buses, certain female volunteers from various continents of the planet also discovered Asi's body. But in 1973 all this came somehow to a dead end. Perhaps, he thought, it was time to get married.

Betty recalls: "I was often asked and, in fact, am still asked today what attracted me to kibbutz life. Was it the sun, the particular food, the laboring men? For me, none of this counted. Many of the things I found in Israel were somehow familiar to me already. Even the presence of soldiers and military vehicles I somehow took for granted. Perhaps images I saw of the Second World War or stories told to me by my parents prepared me for that. From summer jobs back in the Netherlands, I was used by then to hard work, including cowsheds. You must remember that I come from a small northern town where cows, God knows, are quite abundant. What was different for me in coming here was the quality of relationships between people. In Israel I did not find the hypocrisy or social affectation found in Europe—people concealing from each other their true feelings. Here, I found things to be *dugri*, as they say in Hebrew: *straightforward*. If I could not stand the kibbutz administrator, I would tell her so bluntly, without giving a damn. It was difficult because Kfar Yehuda was such a small community, where one had to get along with all the others. The fact I wasn't Jewish did not make things any easier, of course. But on the whole, I felt everyone was much less pretentious.

"At times, it got quite painful. For instance, someone would say to me, 'Isn't it time you went back to Holland? 'or 'You're not even Jewish. Why have you stayed here so long?' But all this remained on the level of family conflicts. It hurt, but you just went on. No deep grudges were held against anyone. The sun, the sexual liberty, or the Biblical ambience—all these were not on my mind at all," she says and laughs. "I've got light skin and can't go out much anyhow..."

Betty came to Israel in 1973, when the country was attacked simultaneously by Egypt and Syria on the Jewish holy day of atonement. Many Israelis attended synagogue on that day or stayed secluded in their homes. She felt that something had to be done to help them. In 1967 she was still too young to be an activist, but during the '73 conflict she was ready to mobilize. By then, for Betty any attack on Jews was an opportunity to atone for what her parents had done or, rather, not done during the German invasion of the Netherlands: namely, saving Jews. She had decided to join Kfar Yehuda as a volunteer. Prior to her trip, Betty was trained as an art therapist but felt like she was made to float in a universe of fairytales and invented theories. Nothing was hands-on, there were just bright watercolor paintings on neat sheets of paper and appointments with frustrated housewives. Working in the kibbutz seemed so much more tangible and obvious: tasks needed completion, and there were no questions to be asked. Relatives and friends of her parents in the north of the Netherlands had warned her that it was risky going to Israel. But Betty replied that it was not as if the issue was riding a motorbike or skiing off-track, it was humanitarian work. Their own children, she said, were the ones taking unnecessary risks, using drugs, alcohol or leading questionable lifestyles.

Betty: "Every activity in the kibbutz, even washing pots and pans or pepper-picking, was meaningful to me: it was the feeling I was part of a bigger event, that I was contributing to a group of people under threat. In Europe anti-Israeli sentiments were on the increase. In the kibbutz only three other volunteers remained: two Dutch girls and a French guy. The two Dutch worked in the kibbutz sheltered-housing units, probably because they knew some German. Older kibbutz members went back to using their mother tongues—Hungarian, Czech or German—oblivious to the fact that thirty years earlier Hebrew was declared the only authorized language. In the kitchen I was happy to have no other Dutch volunteers with me. This encouraged me to learn Hebrew and meanwhile improve my very basic English."

The French volunteer, Didier, worked in the kibbutz tractor maintenance and repair shop, which also integrated into its timetable a number of funny-looking fiberglass Susitas. He was extremely popular with Israeli-born young women, supposedly because he was the sole uncircumcised male in the area. Whether it was out of pure curiosity, or the myth that surrounded non-Jews' performance in bed, or simply the attraction of Didier's long blond hair, it is hard to tell: in any event, in hushed conversations, girls were interrogating each other about the minute details of the *Didier experience*: How exactly does it look or feel? Is the lubrication much improved? etc. etc. Nearly every week, on a sort of rota, another girl would spend time in the men's volunteer room. But Didier turned out to be an odd character, and none of the women chose to remain with him for any length of time. Regardless of the absent circumcision, there was something menacing in Didier's behavior. He spoke broken English with a heavy, almost incomprehensible accent. His conversation didn't only shift gradually from English to French but transgressed rapidly from the real and coherent into the imaginary or, at times, the completely delirious. In the maintenance shop Didier's instability was also noticed after a while, and in the end he was given as sole responsibility the garage compressor, a machine that could not cause great damage, being used mainly for cleaning motors or inflating tractor tires.

For Betty, it became clear that she was in the right place at the right time. She was aware, nevertheless, that things might take a while, what with her being not only a gentile but also non-Israeli and not a kibbutz member. How many categories and subcategories does a person need to overcome in creating their new identity? It was also clear to her that she was dropping all the potential partners for cohabitation whose idiosyncrasies she was averse to. The 1940s type was, in her mind, a weak, calculating collaborator. The 1950s one, a Protestant consumerist. The best her own generation could offer her, she thought, was some hippie intellectual. The 1970s proposition, presently before her, was an Israeli partner. When she met Asi in the culture room/library, he was screening slides he had shot in the Sinai desert. Betty found him somewhat frustrated or depressed. It was far from being love at first sight, as suggested by stories, or even a question of sudden physical attraction. Yet for her, it was all clear: Asi was the person of her life.

Asaf—Asi—was merely okay on various levels, but he was okay on all those levels that were important for Betty. If asked, she could not quite enumerate his qualities, but she summed him up as A.A., supposedly because of his given and family names, Asaf Amir. To her parents, back in the Netherlands, Betty just wrote that Asi was *a double A*, meaning *an ace card, a winner*. On their first night together, both of them felt it was average, and a year after their marriage there was an ascent in their pleasure, with the peak reached around the birth of their children. Afterward, sex played a lesser role in their lives, apparently. Finding out Betty was pregnant, the couple followed Asi's army tactics: *trust your own judgment and waste no time waiting for hierarchical orders*. As soon as Asi's sabbatical was due in 1974, he and Betty flew to Cyprus for a civil marriage. The matrimony was not officially accepted by the kibbutz council, and two years dragged before Betty managed to convert and become an Israeli citizen. Only in 1976 did she become a full-fledged member of Kfar Yehuda. Asi's parents, on the other hand, got used to Betty fairly rapidly, and the birth of the two grandchildren did much to accelerate the process. A big outcry came when instead of sending the toddlers to the common nursery, Asi and Betty kept their children at home. Dror and Yael set the example for other kibbutz children, and senior members were more than surprised when a majority of the kibbutz voted positively the following year for overnight stays at parents' homes. The nursery halls became kindergartens. It took years, though, to finance and build larger apartments that could accommodate enlarged families. Meanwhile, mattresses were piled against the wall, and folding cots made their way into family homes.

The ultimate decision to leave the kibbutz took place only ten years later, when the account with the children's home was finally settled, but its seeds had been germinating all along. Once the so-called kibbutz myth was no longer held sacred, it gradually felt permissible to find faults in a system that did not please everyone. But for Asi, the impulse to leave stemmed from a deeper need. It wasn't just the urge to become a professional photographer, a desire that might have eventually been possible to fulfill within the kibbutz framework, it was a developmental impulse, just like the urge to leave the parental nest, in order to incarnate his own personal identity, perhaps even his full sexual maturity.

Asi: "It took some courage, and much support and assistance from Betty, to get in touch with various fashion magazines, especially the more daring and avant-garde among them. I clearly wished to undertake work with nude models, but in a soft, family like atmosphere. The objective was never pornographic or even *Playboy*-style. After many refusals, I was taken as a trainee by the Dutch journal *The Naked Truth*. The decision fitted us like a glove, as Betty wished to spend time near her parents before the grandchildren became teens. The language, too, played a role. In the Netherlands I was able to get by with English and the little Dutch I picked up through Betty. This kind of arrangement would have been impossible in, say, Italy or France, and in those days the UK was way too conservative. Still, embarking in *The Naked Truth* was like *bang!* as if I had landed from another planet. I was nearly forty and had basic technical skills in photography, but in many ways I had to begin from zero. The European mentality, especially that of a fashion journal, was utterly alien to me. My only chance to survive in that universe was through some kind of adoption. The Dutch photographer, whose assistant I became, was indeed very friendly, but I had to land on firmer ground, make a niche for myself somewhere. This came about through a model named Marieke."

Here Asi needs to mind his words and double-check the effect on Betty of what he says, as he notices her somewhat critical stare. Some details, it seems, will have to be left out of Asi's narrative. At this point I should mention that the three of us are seated in front of the open cafeteria of the Ramat Aviv camping grounds, protected from the sun by large yellow umbrellas.

Betty: "Bigotry is everywhere. It is difficult for people to realize this. Do you know how many Dutch collaborated with the occupier during the Second World War? Even Israelis have the impression that Holland is a friendly nation, with lots of colorful tulips and picturesque windmills. But half of my parents' generation worked with the Nazis, and half of my own generation support the PLO. How many Dutch Jews survived the war? Even Anne Frank was finally betrayed. So what are people going on about? Of the ten percent of Jews that were given shelter? Perhaps another ten percent that got by, using false papers...If I agreed to go back to the Netherlands, at least temporarily, it was mainly for the sake of my parents. There were one or two trivial things that I missed personally, little childhood habits that I longed for. I will admit, as well, that I got tired of worrying constantly, not so much for myself but for Asi and naturally for the children. Every school outing in Israel, every holiday, each school vehicle the children had to use for the regional secondary school, shuttles that were just beginning as we left, all those got to me. It should not be forgotten either that in 1984 buses began being blown up, and the trend of suicide bombs was initiated. Just as 1973 was the right time for me to come to Israel, 1985 was the right moment to take a break and allow the children to breathe freely. I was glad to share with them my own childhood joys, like Madurodam miniature models of the Netherlands, the various zoos and deer parks, and boat rides on the canals."

Putting myself in the reader's shoes, I sense a slight disappointment, or even a reproach, for my failure to deliver the goods, as it were. Instead of elaborating on intimate relations in kibbutz communities, I merely chronicle a couple's mundane existence. My hope was that Asi and Betty's story would be representative enough to illustrate the particular phenomenon of kibbutz mixed couples. While the Amir family is in the throes of departure from kibbutz life, a regression in time will permit a glance into the lives of other Kfar Yehuda volunteers, complementing, perhaps, our topic.

The most dramatic event concerning volunteers in Kfar Yehuda took place during Asi's sabbatical year, in 1975. Didier, the guy from France, was granted Israeli citizenship, a procedure enabled through his mother's Jewish roots. The kibbutz, though, had turned down his application for membership. Worse still for Didier was the fact Dalia G.—one of his bed partners, native of Kfar Yehuda—not only refused his marriage proposal but openly mocked his temerity. Didier's body was found the following day, hanging from an I beam in one of the tractor sheds. In an act that paralleled van Gogh's severed ear, Didier had left an envelope for Dalia G. containing, besides a farewell note—and here, reality just surpasses anyone's imagination—the foreskin of Didier's sexual organ, packed in a bandage and a plastic sandwich bag. Some kibbutz members saw the double act as a heavenly sign, announcing the end of the kibbutz ideal, or perhaps even of Zionism, period.

Other foreign volunteers fared better than Didier, fortunately. Kfar Yehuda statistics indicate sixteen mixed couples, meaning volunteers cohabiting with kibbutz members. Out of those, six eventually left, living elsewhere at present. Three of the ten remaining couples are unmarried. There were also nine children born to single kibbutz mothers, from a relationship with a volunteer. Considering the kibbutz's sixty years of existence, the phenomenon, then, was limited to minor proportions. No known figures were available, though, for the number of children born to female volunteers who left the kibbutz after a short stay there.

Betty and Asi remained twenty years in the Netherlands, and their children now live on their own. To sum up Asi's professional career, suffice it to say that he became a reasonable photographer who perhaps didn't make a name for himself in the fashion industry but managed to make a living from one advertisement project to another, and more as a hobby he developed a minor career as a portraitist and nude photographer of women. During their last year in the Netherlands, an ex-model of Asi, in fact a childhood friend of Betty's, was organizing a number of photo exhibitions of his work in town halls and other public spaces. When their relationship became too intense, Betty put her foot down.

Betty: "We were more or less settled in Groningen, ready to accept that we'd never return to Israel but, to put things figuratively, in the nice green grass there were brambles or evasive thorns. Some of the difficulties were related to my childhood war phantoms or to the weight of anti-Semitism, but others took the shape of underage models or indeed not even very young ones. All of a sudden, I felt rejected, in my own native land. Once the children left home, I became either more sensitive or more perceptive. I told Asi, 'The Holland Kibbutz has to end, or any kibbutz for that matter. Either we are a conventional married couple, or I am moving out to live with my divorced sister in the family home we inherited.' The house had already served me as a shelter in the past, during other moments of crisis. In Holland, especially in the eyes of Arab or Pakistani immigrants, I was perceived as a Jew and an Israeli. Even Dutch friends and neighbors did not consider me as one of them, just a fool or naïve person. This had to do, of course, with all the naked women my husband was taking pictures of and his involvement in the fashion world. The last straw was when one of my best friends hired Asi as a kind of artistic adviser or private consultant. I just had to say *Stop, that's enough*. Now the nude models remain only as some lost paradise for Asi, a habit that is hard to forgo. But we came up with a sort of substitute: the world Nudist and Naturist Association. Whenever circumstances permit and there's some money accumulated in the bank, we make a dash to some European nudist gathering. When it is beyond us, we make do with an Israeli event, like the present one in Ramat Aviv."

My meeting with Asi and Betty takes place, in fact, by an outdoor swimming club rented by the Israeli Nudist Organization, in a gathering intended for older persons, a retired, or nearly retired, international public. Hotel rooms were affordable and the weather great, but the organizers neglected to take politics into consideration. The Gaza Strip was blocked by the Israeli Army, like some airtight lunchbox, and bombing of residential quarters began in earnest. People had nowhere to hide or escape to, entire families ending up buried under the rubble of their own apartments. In an attempted retaliation, Hamas rockets began landing in the center of Israel. Even those tourists who were not too critical of Israeli policies stayed away from the country because of the bombs. Asi and Betty could not handle the expense of airline tickets this year and therefore joined the local event. By now, Asi was working as a freelance photographer but also took up some journalistic responsibilities in an online news and culture site.

Asi: "My dad used to say there were only two real professions: being a lawyer or being a journalist. He, himself, worked as an attorney, before he immigrated. When I was young I played with the idea of becoming a journalist, but the reality of kibbutz life and the fact I was dyslexic meant it all came to nothing. Now, in the digital age and with spell-check software programs, becoming a journalist is much easier. But to be honest, as far as understanding what's going on in the world, either from a professional or a private point of view, I would give myself a zero. I know today probably as much as I knew as a boy. Why do people vote for the Left on one election and for the Right on the next? Why are technology, industry and financial growth viewed positively one day and the following day it is the environment and animal rights that are on everyone's mind? Sentimental love songs make the top of the charts one year, and the following year it is rap and heavy metal. And why are Israelis not accepted as normal people, neither angels nor demons? It is all beyond me."

Betty and Asi, almost simultaneously: "Why can't Israel be taken for what it is? Why are Italy or France allowed to send boatloads of asylum-seekers back to sea—boats with hundreds of refugees on them that will end up sinking—but we, as a state, are not allowed to defend ourselves from the Gazans?"

The conversation depresses me and only adds to my doubts regarding my participation in this odd assembly of people. I was already past my prime. Did I just come here to stare at naked women? Like myself, they were all over forty, although unlike me, many have kept in shape through regular exercise. Was I living from one day to another, like so many of my compatriots, completely engrossed in food, sex and regular flights abroad, finding myself with a monthly overdraft because once again I bought too many CDs, which I hardly listen to?

I decide to leave Ramat Aviv earlier than planned, call up some friends in Zfad to see whether I may spend a few days in the cool mountain air, and hope that I will stick to the diet I have started. Perhaps, I thought, perhaps Asi and Betty's children will learn a thing or two from the course history has taken. They mentioned that Dror, their son, was employed by a humanitarian NGO in South Sudan. If only a girl of Palestinian origin, living in Amsterdam, would join the same project as Dror, they might get to know each other. Like in Betty and Asi's case, two worlds will unite then to create a new one, a bit modified, and a bit improved. No, the Palestinian girl will not convert to Judaism, and Dror will not have to change his religion either, but in the long summer evenings, in their Dutch home, with its very large windows, they will have no fear to declare that they are of Muslim, Jewish or Hottentots background. Perhaps.

Acknowledgments

As the book is being prepared for publication Gaza is under infernal fire.

Kidnapped Israeli children sit next to Palestinian families in makeshift underground shelters.

I pray for the lives of both Arabs and Jews.

In the process of writing and editing the stories I was helped by a number of persons. Let me thank Asaf for suggesting the subject of the novella included. With the language corrections, and style, I was assisted by Vanessa Wells (American English) and Fergus Paton (British English). Typing and uploading the text onto the Internet, as well as dragging me out of numerous linguistic and electronic difficulties were Catherine Barret and Jerome Perrier. Thank you for being there!

Uri Marcus Hes

October 2023.

---

[1]Hagannah was the main Zionist military body, preceding thus the IDF army of Israel.

[2]Kharedim, in Hebrew, or Haredim, ultra-orthodox Jews.

[3]*ca.* 60,000 m^2

[4]David Ohannessian (1884–1953), Armenian ceramicist who settled in Jerusalem in 1918.

[5]Eric Gill (1882–1940), English designer and sculptor.

[6]Both boys and girls are traditionally circumcised in Egypt, but the result of Female Genital Mutilation is much more devastating, of course.

[7]Shavu'ot, or Feast of Weeks, is one of the three biblical Pilgrimage Festivals.

[8]The pre-1967 border is the demarcation line agreed upon between Jordan and Israel, after the 1949 Armistice.

[9]Shlomo 'Cheech' Lahat, a Likud member, was mayor of Tel Aviv between 1974 and 1993.

[10]A *Goy shel Shabbat,* refers to non-Jews employed by observant homes to execute certain tasks proscribed to Jews during the Shabbat day of rest.

[11]Nahal, or *Nakhal,* is an Israeli program combining agricultural, educational projects and military service.

Milton Keynes UK
Ingram Content Group UK Ltd.
UKHW040418200324
439767UK00001B/46